Jessie Fothergill

Oriole's Daughter

A Novel: Vol. II.

Jessie Fothergill

Oriole's Daughter
A Novel: Vol. II.

ISBN/EAN: 9783337053758

Printed in Europe, USA, Canada, Australia, Japan

Cover: Foto ©Andreas Hilbeck / pixelio.de

More available books at **www.hansebooks.com**

ORIOLE'S DAUGHTER

A NOVEL

BY

JESSIE FOTHERGILL

AUTHOR OF

'THE FIRST VIOLIN,' 'A MARCH IN THE RANKS,' 'PROBATION,'

ETC.

IN THREE VOLUMES

VOL. II.

LONDON

WILLIAM HEINEMANN

1893

ORIOLE'S DAUGHTER

CHAPTER IX.

As time went on, and the situation slowly
developed itself, Minna was forced into an
unwilling, annoyed kind of admiration for
Signora Dietrich—the admiration which
one must necessarily experience for a
woman who has a distinct, rounded
purpose in her mind, and who devotes
herself with a single aim to the accom-
plishment of that purpose. Fulvia had
availed herself of Minna's invitation to
come and see her, and presented herself
almost every day : ostensibly to attend

to her birds ; in reality, as they both knew,
to escape from the fear and constraint and
oppression outside, into a more congenial
atmosphere.   It was here that Minna
began to feel that admiration for the
signora already spoken of.

She could not doubt that Fulvia's
mother knew perfectly well how wretched
her daughter was, nor that, when with
Minna, she sought relief from that
wretchedness in, at any rate, occasional
conversations on the subject of her unhappiness.   It would have been very easy
for Signora Dietrich to prevent the intercourse, forbid her daughter to enter
Minna's rooms, put a stop to the whole
thing, at any moment she might choose to
do so.   But she did nothing of the kind,
nor ever made the least objection to the
visits.   She was evidently very sure of
her power, and did not trouble herself
to interfere in small matters.   It angered

Minna, even while she admired it. She was, as has so often been said, not accustomed to be thwarted, and this calm smiling contempt for her influence irritated her extremely.

In a futile kind of way Minna had tried to find out something about Marchmont, wishing she could hear of something so greatly to his discredit that it might impress even Signora Dietrich with his undesirability as a husband for her daughter. In vain ; she did vaguely hear something about him, but nothing that could be called exactly to his discredit—only that he had appeared in London some two years ago, and had there made a not very successful effort to 'get into' society ; that he had been hated intensely for his meanness and vulgarity ; that he had proposed for an English girl of good family, great beauty, and little or no fortune, and had been sent about his business with disdain ;

all of which might be disagreeable for the
gentleman himself, especially if he could not
conquer himself of his habit of stinginess,
but which formed no data on which to go
to Signora Dietrich and say, 'You cannot
possibly let your daughter marry this man.'

If Minna was conscious that the signora
must be aware of the interviews between
herself and Fulvia, and must be unable to
approve of them, there were other thoughts
which it never entered into her head to
think of, but as to which she was destined
to be, later, much enlightened. In the
meantime the winter progressed ; and she
was still at Casa Dietrich, still profoundly
interested in the drama going on there,
still cherishing a spark of hope, founded
on the fact that, as the marriage had not
yet taken place, perhaps it might be,
'somehow or other,' altogether averted.
She forced herself to be smiling and
polite to the *padrona* of the house, hoping

that by studious civility her word, if ever
she should find a chance to put it in, might
carry some weight with it—in which feeble
assumption she merely illustrated the
fact that the wish is father to the thought,
and that she utterly miscalculated her
enemy's nature and capacities.

Fulvia began to look thin and pale,
but, unfortunately, even more beautiful
and attractive in her delicacy than when
she had been in blooming health. Her
great eyes grew more lustrous, her beautiful face gained a charm of haunting,
wistful loveliness, from the very fact
that its rounded contours were changed ;
and the mournful droop of her mouth
was undoubtedly exquisitely beautiful.
Sometimes she cast aside her despondency,
with an effort, perhaps, but completely,
and was her gay old self again, or very
nearly so ; laughed at them all, caressed
her mother, alternately teased and

coaxed Signor Giuseppe till his sorry
expression relaxed and his eyes softened,
and when he ventured to turn them full
upon the girl and study her, as he had
been wont to do, his sadness vanished ;
love and joy shone from his eyes, ' carina
carisssima ' flowed from his lips, and there
was a gleam of happiness once more.
These gleams, it will be understood, never
occurred when Marchmont was present.
Then, Giuseppe either froze into haughty
silence, or worked himself into a fever
of irritated impatience which ended in
his flinging himself out of the house,
and tearing up and down the busy, tortuous
streets till he felt calmer, or—and that
happened oftenest—took himself out of
the way entirely, unable to bear the sight
of Fulvia's uneasy wretchedness, of her
mother's triumphant self-complacency, and
of Marchmont's nauseous attempts at
flattery and love-making.

Signor Giuseppe was indeed a changed and saddened man. Minna pitied him from the depths of her heart, and did her utmost to afford him any silent consolation that lay in her power. She fancied that, to a certain extent, she had succeeded, for he had once or twice called upon her at the studio, in the twilight hour, on his way home from the cares and toils of *l' ufficio*. She had received him with extended hand, a smile of pleasure, a hearty 'You are welcome,' had drawn a chair near to the stove, and he had sat down upon it. The first time he had made some spasmodic attempts at conversation about all kinds of outside things : a crisis in the Ministry, a message from the King, some English war news that had come, and so forth.

These efforts had by-and-by died down into silence, and when he found that this silence did not annoy her, that he was allowed to sit still as long as he liked and indulge it, he had availed himself of the privilege, and passed an hour or two several times a week in her sitting-room or her studio.   Minna made as if she noticed nothing peculiar or unusual in this conduct.   He did not speak of his feelings ; he did not allude to anything that was going on at home.   The second time that he came she was not in her studio, but in the sitting-room, seated at the table drawing.   She did not speak after they had exchanged a *buon' giorno*, but continued her work with diligence, and had almost ceased to be conscious of his presence in the room, when a deep sigh struck on her ear.   Looking up, she perceived Signor Oriole rising from his chair, looking very haggard, very worn, very sad.   He came up to her, essayed a forlorn kind of smile, and said :

'I must go away now, cara signora. Thank you a thousand times for your hospitality.'

'A very small hospitality,' replied Minna gently.

He shook her hand slowly and limply, and, looking at her, said in a slow, sad voice :

'It must be measured by what it is to me, not to you. To me it is much. Signora, I am very unhappy.'

'I know it, Signor Giuseppe,' she said ; 'it grieves me to see it, and I wish I were not so powerless to help you.'

'Ah, you are very good!' replied he, 'good to me and good to the poor child. That is one kind of help. As for any other kind, nothing can give it except an estate, and a banking account larger than those possessed by Signor Marchmont.' He laughed nervously, with a gleam of his old sardonic amusement, and added : 'Will

you let me come again, if you do not find
it quite too annoying ?'

'Come when you please—every day if
you like, if it does the least good.'

'Grazie infinite,' replied poor Signor
Giuseppe, and was gone.

About this time, too, Minna hit upon
another plan for helping Fulvia herself
through some of the weary hours which
she had to pass in her lover's company.
Minna had lost the fervour of delight and
enthusiasm in her work which she had felt
for some little time after she had shown it
to Signor Giuseppe, and explained to him
its origin.   Her hand would not return
with any pleasure to shaping that figure of
youth and strength and life, of happiness
in the midst of toil, which had inspired her
months ago.   She covered it up, wonder-
ing sadly when she would feel fit to return
to it ; and she determined instead to do a
likeness of Fulvia.   In order to accomplish

this purpose, it was necessary to ask her mother's permission, which Minna boldly did.

'Signora, I have a favour to ask of you,' she said one night, as they stood in the hall outside the dining-room when dinner was over.

'Anything in the world that lies in my power. I am your servant,' said the signora, showing her white teeth in a sweet, malicious smile.

'I wish you would let Fulvia sit to me. I am very anxious to do a bust of her, or to try if I can do one.'

'You flatter us both, signora. I find that your amiability makes far too much of my little one. Her head will be turned, but I cannot refuse such a request.'

'Oh, thank you! Then she may come to the studio and give me some sittings?'

'With pleasure. Only—you will excuse me for reminding you that Fulvia is now

betrothed to Mr. Marchmont, who therefore has the first claim upon her time.
He will be enchanted, I am sure, that you
should take her likeness, but at the same
time he will doubtless often wish to be
present when she is sitting to you.'

Minna had been prepared for something
of the kind.

' That I find perfectly natural under the
circumstances,' she said, with unmoved
countenance and undiminished cheerfulness. ' Fulvia can go with me to my
studio, and Mr. Marchmont shall be admitted at whatever hour he likes to call—
when she is there.'

' Then we may consider the matter
settled,' said the signora, with the air of a
great lady graciously bestowing a favour
on a very insignificant person, all of which
Minna felt—felt to the marrow of her
bones, and boiled with indignation at being
thus patronized by that ' creature '; but all

of which she resolutely swallowed, and swallowed with a good grace, for the sake of getting this slight alleviation in Fulvia's distasteful day's duties.

Thus it was arranged. From that day onwards Fulvia accompanied Minna nearly every morning to her studio, and the work of modelling her likeness began. Minna found it a perfectly fascinating occupation. She was never tired of watching the charming head, of causing it to turn this way and that, of trying the effect of different styles of hair-dressing, of different veils or hoods, or draperies cast over the glistening hair, of endeavouring to catch the effect of some fleeting smile, the curve of some dimple, or the steadfast melancholy of the beautiful mouth when sad thoughts had banished from its lips all attempt at a smile. She began models in two or three different attitudes, and was pleased with them all. The figure of the workman was shrouded away from sight. He must be left until better days—till the danger should be over and Fulvia safe and free from the hateful bonds which at present held her.

Marchmont was graciously pleased to approve of the sittings, and to give them much more frequently than they desired the pleasure of his company while those sittings were going on. He was aware that Minna, though visiting very little, did so of her own choice, and that she could, had she so wished, have been a constant guest in some of the most coveted society in Rome. For this reason, if for no other, he approved. He was also fully conscious that she disliked him more than words could express, and that it was only for Fulvia's sake that he was tolerated in these rooms ; so, true to his type, he experienced all the more pleasure in presenting himself repeatedly, and behaving as one who was quite at his ease, boasting, swaggering, and patronizing everyone and everything he came in contact with. They were uncomfortable hours to Minna, those which this creature passed in her sanctum ; it was only Fulvia's quiet but intense gratitude which gave her the patience to continue to receive him.

One morning, when they were all three together, her friend Mrs. Charrington called, came into the studio and sat down. Minna, with great presence of mind, introduced her two visitors—Mr. Marchmont, Signorina Dietrich. Marchmont, who had never yet succeeded in getting an invitation to one of Mrs. Charrington's evenings, and who was convinced that it was entirely owing to the fact that he had so far not made her acquaintance and been able to show her how delightful he was, exhausted himself in attempts to be ingratiatingly polite. With each ill-contrived effort he

merely roused more thoroughly the complete contempt of the cool-headed woman
of the world, who never for a moment betrayed her utter disdain of him—never for
a moment allowed him to gain the faintest
shred of a vantage-ground or possibility of
approaching her any nearer. She replied
with indifferent glacial politeness and a
smile to everything that he said, and she
would certainly cut him dead next time she
met him in the Corso or on the Pincian
Hill.

She measured Fulvia from head to foot
with calm, self-possessed, open curiosity
and interest, and looked from her to the
bust of her which was in progress, put up
her eyeglass, and said :

'Brava, Minna ! You certainly have a
talent, if not a genius, for portraiture. That
is simply admirable. You have a charming
model also—an inspiration in herself.'

She smiled with conventional ·sweetness,

and bowed towards Fulvia, who fixed her large eyes upon her with serious, inquiring earnestness, and did not seem either fluttered or confused, pleased or displeased, by the notice thus bestowed upon her.

'Come and have tea with me this afternoon,' said Mrs. Charrington to Minna, as she rose to go.

'Thank you, but——'

'"But me no buts." If not this afternoon, which? Or, if you can't or won't come to me, tell me when I may come to you. I came not merely to discharge myself of an invitation, but to see that something definite was arranged, because I wish to see you.'

She stood and waited, her eyes fixed with unsparing shrewdness on Minna's face. The latter saw that the interview had to come. The sooner it should be over the better.

'I'll come this afternoon. I can manage it,' she said.

'Very good. And let the tea-hour extend itself to dinner-time and the evening as well. Now that I have you I may as well get all I can.'

'Very well,' said Minna unenthusiastically. 'At five o'clock I'll be with you.'

'Bene! Good-morning!' with a comprehensive and perfectly meaningless bow to Marchmont, and a condescending nod to Fulvia.

'Allow me,' exclaimed Marchmont, opening the door. 'Did you drive? Let me see you to your carriage.'

She made no objection. He went down the stairs with her, and presently returned looking highly satisfied with himself.

'A thoroughly stylish, well-bred person, Mrs. Charrington,' he said approvingly, and Minna repressed a shudder. 'Has she long been a friend of yours, Mrs. Hastings?'

'Ever since I first visited Rome—now eight years ago,' replied Minna dryly. 'Now, Fulvia mia, I release you. We will put on our bonnets and go home to lunch.'

They did so. Minna did not return to her studio that afternoon, but presented herself at the appointed hour, and rang the bell of Mrs. Charrington's *piano*. She found her alone.

CHAPTER X

AFTER tea had been administered, and sundry indifferent matters discussed, Mrs. Charrington said, with a subtle change in her tone :

' My dear, I congratulate you on the company in which I found you this morning !'

' What was wrong with the company ?' asked Minna calmly, but determined to fight.

Mrs. Charrington shrugged her shoulders.

' The girl is perfectly beautiful !' she said, almost irrelevantly. ' I don't wonder that you like to take her portrait ; but what was the other creature doing in your studio ?'

'Unfortunately "the girl," as you call her, is engaged to the other creature ; and he has claims upon her society.'

'She's Signora Dietrich's daughter, isn't she ?'

'Yes.'

'And are you still staying at that place ?'

'I am. It's too much trouble to move.'

'Or, rather, you don't wish to move. I am astonished at you, I must say. It is so unlike anything you have ever been accustomed to.'

'But what do you know about it ? When I told you I was there you said you had no idea who they were.'

'I had not then. But since then I have found out all that is necessary.'

'Very kind of you to take so much trouble. Was it on my account ?'

'Don't be huffy. Do you suppose I had anything but kind intentions towards you? Yes, it was on your account. And also because—though I could not remember just at the moment—I had a glimmering idea that I had once heard something about those people. It is such a bore to have a half-caught fact wandering round in your head, and evading you every time you tried to grasp it, so I just made some investigations. La signora is not the most estimable character imaginable, I think?'

'I should suppose not. I have nothing to do with her—practically.'

'She comes of a very clerical family,' pursued Mrs. Charrington composedly. 'All the women of her family are bigoted devotees, and very shaky as to morals. The two so often go together. Then, there is a man about the place, isn't there?'

'Yes,' replied Minna dryly.

'Yes—exactly. Signor Oriole, or some such name. Oh yes, it is an old story, common enough here, and disreputable enough.'

'He is not disreputable,' said Minna stoutly. 'I am certain of that—though why they are not married now, when there is no husband in the way, I really don't know. It is very unfair to the girl.'

'It is easy enough to know why they are not married. He is, or was, a gentleman. He had a name, and a bringing up. He comes of a good family. He gave up his estate and his time, his youth and his strength, to his country. Then he got entangled with this woman some time or other, when he was wounded, or ill, or something. In a way, he is weak. She is strong all round. He was quite under her fascination for several years—not many, but several. He gave up what few rags

of position and consideration remained to
him, in order to be near her. A miserable
despicable situation for a man of any brains
or cultivation to be in. Her husband had
wretched health. Everyone knew he could
not live. Oriole had every intention of
marrying her, and then it would have been
all right. But, not long before Dietrich's ·
death he discovered that she could be false
to her lover as well as to her husband. In
spite of having, as he gave out, cast away
every shred of the condition of *gentil uomo*
—outwardly, at any rate—there was still a
remnant or two of prejudice left within. He
could not swallow that pill. He would not
marry her. He did not desert her. That was
his mistake and his weakness. She could
have got on perfectly well without him—
such people can always get on, somehow,
because they have no scruples and no
feelings, only passions and greeds of different kinds. They say he is desperately

fond of the child. I don't know how that may be. He has paid dearly enough for his slip, years ago. His life has been simply ruined, neither more nor less.'

'Yes, I know,' said Minna, as composedly as she could. She did not betray the force of the shock with which the news of the true state of things had struck her. It had not occurred to her to imagine it for herself, but now that she heard it thus philosophically set forth by an outsider, the truth of it came irresistibly to the front. That, certainly, accounted for everything. It made the situation more tragic, but to a certain extent it relieved her mind, because it vindicated Signor Oriole.

'I heard at the same time some talk of an engagement between the child and a rich foreigner,' continued Mrs. Charrington. 'I did not quite believe it, but from what you say there appears to be some truth in it.'

'It is only too true. He and the mother are agreed. The girl is helpless, Signor Oriole is helpless, of course. This creature is enormously rich, and has tempted Signora Dietrich with a bait which she cannot resist. He is to pay her debts and give her some money—set her free, in fact—and Fulvia is to be handed over to him. It is a horrible situation.'

'You speak as if you had some personal concern in it,' said Mrs. Charrington in her clear, incisive tones—cool, cutting, merciless. As those tones struck upon her ear, Minna felt how utterly illogical was her own position in the matter, how purely a thing not of reason, but of feeling, impulse, emotion. She realized that she had nothing to urge in her own defence if she should be attacked on the subject, 'and she clung all the more ardently to her attitude in the matter. It was another proof of the friendlessness, the forlornness,

of poor Fulvia Dietrich that people should
wonder why she, Minna Hastings, should
concern herself with her affairs. Of course
there was nothing to be gained by it but
vexation and disappointment, and it is so
foolish, so unspeakably foolish, to let one's
self encounter these things on behalf of
one who can give nothing in return for the
service—wild, quixotic, vain. She said
nothing.

'Don't you think,' continued Mrs.
Charrington, in her most dulcet tones,
'that on the whole you had better get out
of it? It isn't a nice sort 'of thing to be
mixed up in.'

'I am not "mixed up" in it. I have
nothing to do with it. I am sorry for the
poor man who has made such a mess of
his life. I pity the girl beyond all expression. It is pollution for an innocent
young creature to be in the presence, even,
of that man who she is told is to be her

husband.   I confess I can't sit still and see
a helpless thing writhe in torture without
even putting out a hand to try and help.
It is little enough that I can do.   By
coming to my studio for an hour or two
every day she has less time to spend with
him and her mother.   And, so long as she
is not actually married to him, I keep
cherishing a hope that perhaps something
may happen to break it off—if you call
that being mixed up with it.'

'I do,' was the decisive reply. 'Of
course when one sees helpless creatures
being tortured, to use your flowery
language, one must do something.   I
should do something myself.   But that is
just the point.   Why see them ?   Why be
anywhere near them ?   You have plenty
of friends of your own standing, your own
kind, and your own position.   You have
relations and connections.   Why must you
cast them all off, and go and busy yourself

in the concerns of a disreputable Italian woman and her threadbare old simpleton of a former lover, and their child and the vulgar little upstart who wants to marry the child. " A passion in tatters " on the part of the two elderly persons—a stupid vulgar love-story on that of the younger ones. Do look at it in the proper light. What have you to do with such things— what do you want *dans cette galère?* You can't do anything, as you say. Go away and leave them, and return to your natural place amongst your friends and in society. That is the only course for you to take.'

Minna shook her head.

' I'm interested in it,' she replied.

Mrs. Charrington began to look vexed.

' I don't think you understand what a mistake you are making.'

' And I am very fond of the child,' pursued Minna. ' The more I see of her the more I love her. Poor thing ! I can't understand how any woman with a heart in her breast, seeing what is going on, could stand aside and leave her to her fate, without even a word of sympathy.'

'Oh, when it comes to "a woman with a heart in her breast," that is just the same as when philanthropists and charitable or religious maniacs tell you they "feel" something very strongly. They "feel" that Mrs. Brown or Mrs. Jones, and her crew of begging children, must not be allowed to go to the workhouse or prison, and——'

'Really, Mary, your similes are flattering!'

'There is too much truth in them. The plain fact of the matter is that you have got into a set of anything but respectable people, whose youthful follies and sins are coming home to roost, and bringing their children in their hands with them. You ought to have nothing whatever to do with them. You are letting yourself be carried away by your " feelings." Oh, I could say many rude and true things on that subject. Some day or other you will bitterly repent it. When that day comes don't say that I did not warn you.'

'It may come, then,' said Minna, with a heightened colour. 'I am satisfied with what I am doing. I wish it were more; I should embrace it with eagerness. If I could get Fulvia Dietrich out of this horrible situation, at almost any cost to myself I would do it. I was not quite sure what I felt about it before, but your plain-spoken remarks have made my own mind quite clear to me. So don't you think we have said enough about it ?'

'I see it is useless to say anything more to you,' replied Mrs. Charrington, disguising her vexation at having thus overshot her mark, as she now plainly perceived she had done. 'I have relieved my mind, at any rate, and discharged what I felt to be an imperative duty. It hasn't been pleasant, and I am aware that it is the kind of thing one never gets any thanks for. I have no objection to talk about something else, as you have taken the bit between your teeth.'

They did not return to the subject. Mrs. Charrington exerted herself to play the amiable hostess, Minna was the complaisant guest; but she felt all the time that Mrs. Charrington was disapproving, deeply disapproving, and the intercourse was constrained and unsatisfactory.

When Minna went away, 'Remember,' said her friend, 'I decline to call upon you at that house. I shall look you up at the studio now and then, but I don't countenance Casa Dietrich.'

'How pleasant it would be if we could crush out all pain and wrong and wickedness by simply saying we did not countenance them!' was Minna's retort, in a tone not devoid of bitterness. 'Good-night,' she added, and went out and down the stairs. She breathed a long sigh as she got into a little carriage, and gave the address of Casa Dietrich.

' She will never understand and never approve,' she said to herself. ' And it will be the same with everyone I know. They will call me mad and a simpleton. Well, they will just have to call me so. What would it matter if Fulvia were happy? How I wish she was my daughter! I wish I had a daughter.'

CHAPTER XI.

ON the following morning, just as Minna was preparing to go out to her studio, there came a tap on the door, followed by the entrance of Fulvia.

'I am so sorry, signora,' said she. 'Mamma has sent me to say that I shall not be able to go with you to-day. We are to go out, she and I, and Signor Marchmont. We shall be out all day, and we shall be busy for several days.'

She spoke listlessly and mechanically, without a trace of spirit or animation.

'Oh, I am sorry. What makes you so busy?'

'My trousseau,' replied Fulvia coldly.

' Your trousseau ? Why—has there— is anything settled ?'

' I am to be married in the middle of April—in a month from now. And it seems I am to be dressed up for it, like our Blessed Lady for a *festa*.'

She looked drearily round the room ; her face was pale, her lips looked drawn and dry. She went up to the cage where the canaries now flourished exceedingly in the comfort of Minna's room, and on the good food which she gave them, and mechanically brushed some grains of seed from the cloth into her hand, dropped them into the fender before the stove, and stood there as if not knowing what to do next.

Minna also did not know what to do, and was filled with impotent rage at her own want of power or inventiveness, or whatever it might be. The dreadful thing was coming nearer and nearer, and not a glimpse appeared in their horizon of any weapon or means of warding it off. After a moment's pause, during which all kinds of wild ideas and speculations rushed through her brain, Minna asked abruptly :

'Fulvia mia, tell me something. I have a good reason for asking you. When you first told me of this thing, you said your mother was in debt, and that Mr. Marchmont was going to pay her debts.'

'Yes, it is quite true,' Fulvia nodded. 'I heard them talking about it. I heard him tell mamma that she was the hardest-hearted business woman he had ever met, and that she would wring blood from a stone.'

Minna refrained from comment, and went on :

'Did you ever hear how much money your mother wanted to pay her debts ? Is it a great deal ?'

'Oh, an enormous sum !' cried Fulvia.

'At least ten thousand lire. I heard them say so. And then he gives her a present as well, but more than that—far more. I do not know how much.'

Minna almost smiled at first, and then felt a sense of burning rage at the idea conveyed to her by Fulvia's words. The girl was then to be sold for a beggarly four hundred pounds, more or less. So much was necessary, it would seem, to set Signora Dietrich free from embarrassment. The rest was simply for luxury, was over and above, was the premium on her daughter's wretchedness and degradation. Minna meditated darkly. She felt restless, feverish with anxiety and the agitation of a half-formed scheme which had just begun to shape itself in her mind.

There was a pause. Then she said :

'Well, cara mia, I am sorry you cannot come to me, but I fear there is no getting out of this expedition.'

'Oh no !' said Fulvia apathetically. ' I only came to tell you of it. A rivederci.'

She smiled faintly and drearily, and went away.

Two or three days passed, during which Minna scarcely saw anything of the three chief actors in the drama. She was left much to her own devices, and 'thought the more.' The weather was mild and exquisite ; they were out all day, now buying things, now off on some excursion or ' pleasure ' party. There was a subdued bustle about signora's rooms, as of dressmakers, milliners and other purveyors of feminine finery and luxury. It was quite evident that things were being hastened on to their end. Meantime, the everyday prosaic business of the *pensione* went on as usual. The house was full. It was the height of the season in Rome. Every day people came and went. Every day Signor Oriole looked

more and more busy, more and more
shabby, woebegone, and irritable. Need-
less to say that he never formed one of any
of the parties or excursions. He went on
in a sort of mechanical way, grinding at
the wretched duties which he had taken
upon his shoulders long ago ; working out
his punishment, and, so far as Minna could
judge, and much to her astonishment, not
rebellious, only miserably resigned.

Minna did little work during those days,
though she passed a good deal of time
at her studio. She was utterly absorbed
in anxious considerations of a kind perfectly fatal to the abstraction required for
artistic work.

Thus things stood when one afternoon
she sat up in her parlour at Casa Dietrich,
with a book idly lying on her knee, as
she gazed out into the clear cold afternoon
light, which would soon descend into
darkness and night.

A knock on the door. In answer to her 'Avanti,' Fulvia entered.

'Ah, Fulvia, come in. It is ever so long since I saw you.'

'Good-evening, signora. I only came to look at my birds,' said Fulvia in a low voice. 'I have neglected them shamefully, but I am sure you have not.' She went up to the cage and chirped to them. 'There is nothing for me to do,' she said with a faint smile.

'All the better. You have been busy. Come here ; sit down on this sofa and tell me how you are.'

Fulvia accepted the invitation, sat down, and stretched out one hand towards the warmth that came from the stove, from which also came a dull, pleasant red glow. The room was warm and pleasant, scented with violets and early roses.

'It is so delightful here,' said Fulvia, rather wearily.

' It is delightful to see you there. But you have been very busy, I suppose ?'

' Oh, I suppose so. We have rushed from one place to another. We have seen a great many things, and a great deal of money has been spent. I am quite be-wildered with it. And I have tried on so many clothes. All day, when I was not having them bought for me, it seems to me that I was standing there with a woman pinning and fitting, and clipping things with great scissors. Some of them are ready, and have come home.'

' But you do not wear them !' said Minna, whose eyes fell upon the girl's dress, and saw that it was the old, much-despised blue woollen thing which Fulvia had worn when she had first met her.

' No ; I will never put any of them on till I am obliged to,' said Fulvia sullenly.

They were both silent for a little while, till Fulvia, presently leaning forward on

the sofa, and clasping her hands round
her knees, said :

' Signora !'

' Yes ?'

' Mamma says I am to be married in
three weeks.'

' So soon ?'

' Sometimes I think it is awfully soon.
Then, again, I have another feeling, which
is, that three weeks may mean—never.
I have such strange sensations in my
mind. I hardly know how to explain them
to you. I feel as if the time would go
on and on, and all this foolish making of
dresses, and buying of jewellery might
go on too, till the time comes, and that
then I shall not know anything more,
but shall somehow be away, out of it all,
flying about in space ; as if I should have
become something else—not a girl—not a
human creature any more. I shall be free
from all this pain and fear, and from all

this weight which seems to be bound on to my head, and round it ; but at the same time, I shall have forgotten all the things I used to know. I shall not remember any more what the earth was like, or what Rome was. All the dreadful things will be forgotten—but all the good things too. For instance, I should have forgotten mamma and Signor Marchmont, as if I had never known them; but I should have forgotten you too, and Beppo. I do not wish to forget you, and to forget Beppo would mean to forget all the greatest happiness I have ever had.'

'You must not indulge in such fancies. Grief and joy always go together here. You will not forget us, any more than we shall forget you.'

'For the last few days, Signor Marchmont has talked about what "we" shall do when we are married,' pursued Fulvia, unheeding Minna's futile remark. 'He

has kept asking me questions, and expecting answers to them. It was dreadful
before, when I only had to listen, but now
—to have to answer these questions is
frightful. If I could be silent always—
if I were quite sure that I should never
need to speak a word again, I think I
could go through anything. But this
talking—my head feels so strange!' she
added, putting her hand up to it. 'Do
you think I shall be able to bear three
weeks more of this, without something
happening? Don't you think something
is sure to happen before then?'

Minna, speechlessly, put out her hand to
take that of Fulvia, and while she held it
and sought wildly in her soul for something
that might carry comfort, she saw all at
once that a change had come over Fulvia's
face—a stiffness into her attitude. The
hand was cold, the face was white. She
evidently neither heard nor saw anything

more, and her figure began to sway when she stood, for she had risen from her seat while describing her sensations to Minna.

The latter sprang from her chair, caught her in time to prevent her falling, and half pulled, half led her toward the sofa, and got her on to it. There she lay, in a dead faint.

'Now is my time,' said Minna to herself. 'I should be a criminal if I were to hesitate any longer;' and with that, after casting one hasty look towards Fulvia, she left the room, and sped along the corridors as fast as she could go till she came to Signora Dietrich's room. She knocked loudly and unceremoniously on the door, opened it and confronted the signora, who was writing at a table, and who had just lifted her head to see what the interruption was.

'Signora, your daughter is ill. She is fainting. She is in my room. You had better come to her at once!' said Minna;

and without waiting for a reply, she flew
back to her own quarters, where she found
Fulvia exactly as she had left her.

Scarce two minutes had passed since
she had left the room. She scarcely had
time to dash some water on the girl's face,
when a step behind her—a light but
audible footstep—warned her that Signora
Dietrich was in the room. She closed the
door with deliberation, came up to the
couch, and looked upon the rigid form of
her daughter.

'What is all this?' she asked, but without any excitement or irritation in her
manner. 'What has she been doing? She
appeared quite well when we came in at
four o'clock.'

'No—she is not well. No one is, or can
be well, who is so unhappy as she is,' replied
Minna openly.

'She is not unhappy,' replied the signora,
still calmly and deliberately. 'She is fanci-

ful, she is ignorant, and she is young. She has always been so much petted and indulged. It is constantly the case. She thinks, before she is seventeen, that she knows better than her mother, who is forty-seven, what is for her good and happiness. I thought exactly the same when my mother married me to Signor Dietrich.'

She was undoing Fulvia's dress, with skilful and not unkindly hands ; but there was no pity, no sympathy, no unbending in her attitude.

'And do you feel now that you were wrong, and that your mother was right ?' asked Minna, beside herself.

Signora Dietrich paused for a moment in her operations, and looked Minna full in the face.

'Certainly I do,' she replied, and fell to work again.

'A lie,' said Minna to herself. 'She

did not even get material prosperity from the bargain.'

'Did you suffer thus?' she asked again, and her eyes once more fell upon Fulvia's white, rigid, unconscious face.

'Girls are hysterical,' was the signora's reply. 'There, she is better now. She was tired. We have had a busy day. I must tell Marchmont that she must keep quiet to-morrow.'

'I should advise you to keep her out of his way as much as possible for the next three weeks, if you wish your plan to be accomplished. She has had about as much as she can bear.'

'You are extremely kind, thus to interest yourself in my poor affairs,' said the signora blandly, in her full musical tones. 'I am glad to have this opportunity of thanking you for your disinterested kindness.'

Minna felt the insult that was implied.

but she had her end to gain. She was not to be turned aside from it by a few amenities of this description. So she replied, as if she had not noticed the tone at all :

'Fulvia is dear to me. I love her, and wish her to be happy. Is she not recovering a little now ?'

'Yes. She is going to be better, I think.'

'It is dark. I will light the lamp,' said Minna, and she did so quickly. The light was a good one, and served amply to illuminate the scene and those taking part in it.

By slow degrees the rigidity gradually left Fulvia's face and limbs. A long, shuddering sigh broke from her breast, and her eyes slowly opened. They fell at once upon her mother, who was standing near her. Signora Dietrich, despite her impecuniosity, dressed well when once she had made up her mind to get out of her dressing-gown into her gown. She had on just now a handsome black satin garment, with a white lace collar and cuffs. The somewhat florid and profuse style of her jewellery was the only 'mark of the beast' to distinguish her.

'Mamma!' exclaimed Fulvia, starting up, and looking round her in a bewildered way. 'Where am I, and what has been the matter with me?'

'Little over-tired, that is all,' answered her mother. 'You've had a little faint, as girls will sometimes, when they are excited or exhausted. Do you feel fit to walk now? Because, if so, we will relieve Signora Hastings of our presence, and let her have her room to herself.'

Fulvia made no reply. Her face was still very white, and a strange hollowness had come under her eyes and in her cheeks.

'Pray do not hurry,' said Minna. 'I should like to say something to you, signora,' she continued earnestly. 'Will you not sit down here? I mean no disrespect to you by anything I may say. Pray remember that.'

Signora Dietrich bowed with cold dignity, and waited. She even took the chair which Minna offered her. The latter went on :

'I am sure you wish your daughter's happiness.'

'It would be very unnatural if I did not—my only child,' replied the lady, but still coldly.

'And you think to secure it by marrying her to a rich man?'

'It is not necessary for me to explain what I think. It is absurd to think we have secured anything, by any arrangements we can make. We can but act for the best, and await the result. You have

lived long enough in our country to know
that our marriage arrangements and our
ideas upon these questions are quite
different from those which prevail in yours,'
said madame, with a scarcely concealed
sneer. 'I thank the good God that it is
so. I may be prejudiced, but I prefer the
absolute obedience to parents, and the
retiring modesty which characterizes the
young girls of my country, to the boldness
and forwardness which one sees in the
English, and more so, if possible, in the
Americans,' said Signora Dietrich, clearly
and calmly. 'I have repeatedly heard
that no harm comes of the freedom you
accord your girls. I do not believe it. I
have seen many of them, sitting round my
own table, as well as in public places and
in my friends' houses. There is a hardi-
hood, a boldness, a masculine roughness,
about them which is hateful to me,' she
went on, with what was evidently the most

sincere and intense conviction. Minna saw that she was telling the truth now, at least.

'They walk alone in the streets,' pursued the signora. 'No girl can do that without bad consequences. It is simply impossible. I do not blame the girls. I pity them. They did not make the institutions of their country, and are not answerable for them ; but if they knew what graces would be added to them, how much they would gain in charm and attractiveness, had they but the modesty and bashfulness of our own Italian girls, they would of their own accord refuse to do the things which we find so atrocious. Once for all, signora, understand that I know the customs of our countries are different, and that I prefer those of my own. In your country a girl is said to choose for herself— a husband, I mean. The result is, there are more unhappy old maids in England

than in any other country on the face of
the earth. Perhaps they enjoy themselves,
or think they do, in the exercise of their
freedom, while they are still young and
the world is fair to them ; but they repent
it bitterly afterwards, and I have heard
more than one truth-speaking English
mother wish that there was something
more like our system prevailing at home.
In your country you arrange marriages
secretly and often unsuccessfully, because
it is considered a shame for it to be
acknowledged that a girl wants a husband.
With us it is an acknowledged fact that
only through having a husband can she
gain any position. Ours is the more
honest method of the two. An unmarried
woman is here an anomaly ; her position is
wretched, her privileges *nil*. It is the
duty of every good mother to provide
early against the possibility of any such
lot befalling her daughter. As much her

duty,' continued the signora with emphasis, 'as to bring her up to be modest and virtuous. Do that while she is still a child. When she is older give her a husband. It is the law of God and the law of nature, and it is commanded by the Church, in the majority of cases, that a woman should be a wife and mother ; and a child's fancies must not be allowed to interfere with the performance, by her mother, of the most sacred duty. Love, obedience, self-sacrifice, these are woman's duties, her privilege, her happiness. My Fulvia shall not have the path to them closed, and by her own mother. Excuse this long dissertation on my part. I fancy you were going to say something, and I am prepared to give it my full attention, from politeness—the politeness which is habitual in our country—not because you have any right to utter a word in the matter.'

'Yes ; I had something to say,' replied Minna, refusing to be befogged by madame's eloquence, though she saw that the author of that eloquence believed firmly in every word she spoke. She was convinced that the act she contemplated was for Fulvia's good, as well as to her own advantage, and this conviction, of course, made it more difficult to argue with her.

'This is what I had to say,' Minna went on, after pausing to draw breath. She spoke curtly, plainly, and almost roughly. 'You have selected for your daughter's husband a man whom she loathes. He is not her countryman. He has no such ideas as those you have just been speaking of. He is rich, but he is not even a gentleman. He is a vulgar, purse-proud, mean upstart. He is not in society; his manners are too odious and his stinginess too great to admit him there. Your daughter will

not even gain a position by marrying him.
He proposed to a young Englishwoman
who, happier than your daughter, was able
to decide for herself in the matter, and
who rejected him with contempt. Had he
ventured to address her again, her brothers
would probably have horsewhipped him—
as he deserved. He is a coward. He,
knows that Fulvia detests him, and he
shelters himself behind your authority,
which can compel her to the hateful
marriage with him. All his money cannot
make him anything but detestable to a
modest and pure-minded girl—like your
little Fulvia,' she added, with a slight
break in her voice, as she laid her hand
for an instant on the girl's wrist. ' You
are not doing your duty by her. You are
committing a hideous sin in tying what
you yourself call a modest and virtuous
girl to that—bah ! I should have no right
to say these things to you if I had not

something to propose as an alternative.
You say you love your daughter. In that
case, I suppose you are willing to make
some sacrifice for her sake, and to secure
her happiness. I hear that Mr. Marchmont is to relieve you from all money
embarrassments. If I were a rich woman,
I would say, " Take twice as much from me
as he gives you." But I am not rich. I
am only moderately well off. All I can
propose is this : If you will release Fulvia
from her engagement, I will provide for
her both now and in the future. At
present I will take the whole expense of
her maintenance from you. If she should,
later, meet a man whom she could love,
and who should wish to marry her, I will
pay her every year half of my income ;
and I will at once make a will, leaving my
entire property to her at my death. I am
mistress of all that I have, and as my
family are well off, they need not be

injured by my taking this course. Fulvia need never fear care or want if you will agree to this arrangement ; and if she will give me continually the affection she feels for me at present, and is restored to the happiness which is her right at her age, I shall be more than repaid. I shall be rich. This is what I offer you. I am aware that it does not much improve your position, except through your daughter's happiness ; but as I imagine that to be your main object in life, I shall knów by your acceptance or refusal of my proposal whether what you say about this is true, or simply an excuse to get what you want for yourself, not for her.'

'Signora !' cried Fulvia, 'signora ! Oh, if I might die for you at this moment ! Mamma ! mother ! speak — let me be happy again !'

Her voice broke into a wail, as she turned from Minna and looked at her mother.

Signora Dietrich had not for a moment
lost her presence of mind. She could hit
hard, and she could also take hard knocks,
unperturbed. She looked from one to the
other of them, calmly, gravely, unwaver-
ingly. Her voice, when she spoke, was
sweet and strong ; she threw over her
features an expression of resignation, half
sad, half bitter.

' I see,' said she, ' that you are, like
most Englishwomen, straightforward, if
somewhat brutal in your way of displaying
even your kind feelings. Your remarks
about my future son-in-law are unwarrant-
able and quite without foundation. Your
offer, however, shows you to be sincere
and well-meaning. You have, I believe,
never been a mother, so you cannot be
expected to understand what one who is a
mother feels, on being asked to discard
her own careful plans for her child's happiness, and to adopt the views of a foreigner,

a complete stranger, unacquainted with her
history and her circumstances, and utterly
unable to appreciate what she is doing in
the matter.   But I love my child, and this
gives me patience.   I wish for my child's
happiness far, far more than for my own,
and this endows me with strength to un-
fold a story of sorrow about which I
should have preferred to keep silence.   I
have educated my daughter in the right
way.   I am quite confident in the stability
of my teaching and of the principles I
have instilled into her mind.   I see that
her ideas have been disturbed, her filial
piety has been tampered with, her unreasoning girlish fancies have been fostered,
without regard to any rights or feelings of
mine.   It is my duty as a mother and as a
Christian to meet this heavy trial with firm-
ness and meekness.   I am not afraid.
Mia figlia, you have heard what Signora
Hastings has said to me ?'

'Yes, mamma,' was the breathless response.

'Good. Then hear now what I have to say to Signora Hastings and to you. I will place the two situations before you, and you can choose between them. I have no doubt as to which course you will pursue.'

She paused for a moment, and then, with solemnity, and sweetness too, which extorted from Minna an unwilling admiration, she proceeded :

'Fulvia mia, I must touch upon topics which it is best that young girls should know nothing about. Signora Hastings has driven me to this painful position by her no doubt well-meant meddling in a matter which she does not understand. You will soon be a wife, and your eyes could not much longer remain closed to much that is sad and evil in this world. You have always been to me a sweet and

obedient child, and, but for this unhappy
interference of a stranger in our affairs, I
believe you would have been the same in
this case as in all others. My daughter,
have I ever treated you with unkindness?
Recall all you can remember of your child-
hood and youth, and tell me, do you
recollect any unkindness from me to
you?'

'No, mamma. You have always, until
now, been good to me—kind and indul-
gent.'

'Until now. That is, it seems to you
that now I am no longer kind and indul-
gent. But has it never occurred to you
that perhaps you did not quite understand
all that I am doing?'

Fulvia was silent. She was still seated
on the sofa, looking white and miserable.
Signora Dietrich had placed herself beside
her, and she now proceeded :

'My child! I know even more of your

recent thoughts than you suppose. In
your short life you have had little sorrow
and much joy—no deceptions, no disappointments. In mine, which seems to me
a long one, I have lived through grief and
bitterness of which you can form no con-
ception. I pass over that for the present.
Just now I ask you only one question,
but I ask it solemnly, and I bid you reply
to it with absolute truth and candour.
Never mind if you hurt me. I know what
your answer will be if you speak the
truth. On your honour, then, of all those
who surround you, and whom you know—
of all your friends, all your relations, not
excepting me—whom do you love the
most?'

Fulvia was troubled by this question,
and did not immediately reply to it. Her
hands moved nervously; her face grew
red, and then pale again. But at last,
raising her eyes, which were filled with a

tender light, she looked full at her mother,
and in a very low but perfectly audible
voice replied :

' Beppo, my mother.'

Signora Dietrich bowed her head gravely
and assentingly.

' Yes,' she observed. ' I am glad to find
you so truthful. I knew this, and have
long known it. We do not always bestow
our greatest love on the most worthy
objects. But I have known this thing,
and though it has many a time lacerated
my heart, I have not spoken of it nor
reproached you with it. But the time,
however, has now come in which I must
speak. My kindness to you, my good intentions towards you, have been called in
question. Though I have absolute right
to dispose of you as I please, without
explaining or justifying myself, I do not
choose to do so. Your mother is weak
where her child is concerned—as she was

once, in far other circumstances, weak before, to her cost.   Fulvia——'

She rose from her place beside her
daughter, and stood before her.

They both had to look up to her.   For
a moment she preserved silence, then said,
in a distinct, unfaltering voice :

' Signor Oriole is your father.'

Minna, though she had so long known
this thing, felt her heart spring to her
throat.   Her emotion caused her physical
agony.   She sat silent, her fingers unconsciously tightening themselves, and clutch-
ing at her dress.   And she watched breath-
lessly.

There was a short silence, during which
Fulvia stared, as if fascinated, at her mother,
with wide-open, frightened eyes and a dazed,
bewildered expression.   Then suddenly she
buried her face in her hands, as if she could
no longer bear to look upon what she saw.
But she was silent still.   Presently Signora

Dietrich, in the same unbroken voice, went on :

' This was your mother's weakness. This is your mother's sin. Now you may judge your mother, if you choose. She can have nothing to answer you. She is at your mercy. She has been punished. Women are made weak, and then are punished for not being strong. One hard punishment of mine has been that the man to whom I gave my whole heart, my whole soul, every-thing that I had to give—this man has never made me his wife. Do you suppose that was not hard for a proud woman to bear? Even after nothing stood in the way—even after I had humbled myself with tears and prayers for your sake—to ask him for this deed of justice, he refused it to me. My other punishment—and I swear it has been the harder of the two to bear—has been that I had to live my life day by day and see that my child, whom I adored, loved this man better than she loved me. The heart and the soul must be strong which can go on with such a life and not succumb to the wretchedness of it. It pleased God to make me strong in these respects — yes, to give me the strength even to tell you this story. Now, my daughter, speak! What have you to say to your mother? Choose between me and your new friend.'

Fulvia uncovered her face. Minna was surprised at its expression. It had aged, but there was no more any indecision, any pleading, any look of submissive dependence in it. She, too, rose, made a step towards her mother, and, looking at her, said :

' Before I tell you that, tell me why, if Beppo was as bad as you say, and treated you with cruelty, you stayed in the same house with him? Why did you let him stay here and work for us—for you and me—as I know he has done?'

Almost without hesitation, and certainly without the flicker of an eyelid, the signora replied :

'For the same reason that has dictated all my other conduct—for your sake. Alone, I was unequal to the responsibility —the wear and tear of carrying on this house. When one has no money and no friends, and when one is alone, one may drown one's self. When one has one's child to live for, one lives through every degradation. That is the reason why I live under the same roof with him.'

Fulvia bowed her head, smiling with indescribable bitterness.

'I see,' said she. 'For me you have endured these sufferings—meaning that, when my turn came, I should suffer, too, and should set you free?'

'I had hoped that it would be your

pride and pleasure to do so,' replied her
mother ; 'and I am confronted with the
extraordinary statement that you are not
in love with the man who wishes to marry
you.   What girl—what decent, virtuous,
well-brought-up girl—is ever in love with
her   husband   when   she   marries   him ?
What should you know of love ?   Heaven
forbid that at your age and in your circum‾
stances you should be acquainted with it.
You know now exactly how things stand.
Now   and   on   the   spot   you   must   make
your decision.   Either your engagement
to Signor Marchmont must be honourably
carried out, in which case I must hear
no   more   sighs   and   complaints,   or   you
must tell me at once that you prefer to
accept Signora Hastings' offer and go over
to her.   Should you thus decide I shall
not reproach you, I shall not blame you.   I
shall simply say, You cease to be my child ;
and I shall require that you both leave my

house this night. Here I take my seat.
Reflect as long as you please on the matter;
but you will give me your answer before
we leave this room.'

She seated herself, folded her hands
on her knee, and waited. Not a tremor
betrayed that she felt any agitation.

Minna confessed to herself that the
woman was magnificent in her cleverness
and audacity. She was playing for what
to her were the highest stakes imaginable
—money, ease, freedom. She was secure
of victory. There was no hope now for
the other side. Minna dared not look
at Fulvia, but, as the girl had not yet
spoken, she made a last forlorn effort,
and said in a rather loud, spasmodic
voice, which broke in discordantly upon
the silence :

' Signora Dietrich, you are acting
unfairly. You ought not to require your
daughter's answer without having called

Signor Oriole, and given him the chance
of replying to your accusations.'

'An Englishwoman, then, in such a
moment as this would lie, would she?'
retorted the signora with unbroken calm ;
but her eyes plunged themselves into those
of Minna with a look of hatred which the
other never forgot. 'Of course you are
Signor Oriole's advocate. His devoted
attentions to you deserve some reward.
I am of course ignorant as to how you
are in collusion in this attempt to divide
me and my child.'

Minna received this unexpected back-
handed stab with great presence of mind ;
looking her adversary full in the face the
whole time ; but there was a strange, whirl-
ing sensation in her head, the like of which
she had never felt before.

'You have accused him behind his
back. You bid your daughter choose,
without letting him tell his side of the

story. You have not told her all,' she added, fixing her eyes ever more resolutely on the signora's face.

For one instant Signora Dietrich's eyes wavered, flickered—for one instant her lips twitched. Then she looked herself again. It was at this moment that Fulvia's voice was heard.

' I hear what you both say,' she observed. ' I have heard all that is needful. Mamma is quite right. The choice must be made now. Suppose she called Beppo, and told all this story over again. Do you suppose I want to see poor Beppo more unhappy than he already is ? Some people are born to be happy, and some to be miserable ; I know now what I have to expect. I should be unhappy now, either way. I should be unhappy now, even with you, signora carissima.' She looked at Minna. 'The more I feel myself justified in accepting your generosity, the more unhappy

I should be, because one must feel one's friends to be very wicked before one can leave them all and go away with a stranger. I will not do that. But I love you for being willing to let me come to you. The other unhappiness is perhaps not greater ; it is different, that is all. I take it. That is my choice. I only ask one thing of you.'

She turned to her mother, and they could both see that a subtle change had come over her. Her eyes looked straight into those of Signora Dietrich, but without any expression, coldly, stonily ; and her attitude took a certain rigidity, she drew herself back as it were. ' Let everything go on without change, as quickly as possible, and do not let us ever speak of this again. It is over—it is done with. Do you understand ?'

' Perfectly, carissima mia. You have taken the wisest resolution imaginable.'

said her mother, rising, and pressing a kiss upon her forehead. ' I knew,' she added, with a sweet smile, ' that the lessons I had so diligently inculcated could not be without fruit, sooner or later.'

' Then we can go,' said Fulvia, who had all in a moment lost her childish retirement of manner, and who now spoke as if she were the person to order how things should be. ' I wish to speak one word with Signora Hastings,' she added ; ' do not be afraid to leave me with her. I shall follow you in a moment. Everything is quite decided now.'

Signora Dietrich went away with a gracious smile. When she had rustled away and they were quite alone, Fulvia turned to Minna, and said :

' What I told you was true. I will not go with you, because there would be no good and no happiness in it. It is

better to be unhappy because of others
than because of one's self. But do you
think I believe that Beppo is a bad man ?'

Her eyes flashed fire as she asked the
question with energy, and with almost
solemn earnestness went on :

'No, he is not bad. There is something bad behind it all—something so bad
that I do not want to know it. But he is
not bad. Signora,' she bent to Minna,
and whispered passionately in her ear, ' I
am *glad* he is my father. It is the one
good thing I have heard to-night.'

She then gave Minna a hasty kiss on
the cheek and one on the hand, and in a
moment Mrs. Hastings was alone. Quiet
though the interview had been, there was
now a singing in Minna's ears, a rushing
noise in her head, and a tremulousness in
her throat, with a general feeling of
collapse and *bouleversement* which told
how strong had been the excitement, and

how intense the strain of the whole episode.

'And she has conquered, and she does not care a straw ; she has got what she wants,' Minna muttered between her teeth, and then tears of rage and disappointment came to her relief. She wept till she was weary, and all the excitement had evaporated.

CHAPTER XII.

It was Fulvia's wedding-day. Some days before Minna had had most of her belongings removed to a couple of rooms which she had taken. She felt it utterly impossible to .remain in the house after the event should have taken place, and would gladly have left, but, on saying something of the kind to Fulvia herself, she had noticed a look of alarm and disappointment pass over her face and dilate her eyes. That was enough for Minna ; but as well as that she had the half-superstitious feeling that even at the very last second something might happen to avert the catastrophe.

Nothing had happened ; nothing was going to happen. Minna, on this unhappy day, left the house early, not intending to return to it. She had said good-bye to Fulvia the night before. As for Signor Giuseppe, she had scarcely caught so much as a glimpse of him for many days. The man contrived to hide and efface himself, as it were. Sometimes Minna was aware of a kind of slender dark shadow slipping away in the background, silent, rapid, noiseless. Once or twice she had tried to lay hold of the shadow, to say a few words to it. to force it to speak to her, but she had not been successful. She had a painful, deep conviction that Signor Giuseppe was suffering horribly ; that he had probably used every persuasion, every argument that he could think of. to persuade Signora Dietrich to abandon her purpose, and that his utter failure to move or turn her aside had literally crushed him.

The thought of this helpless misery made Minna suffer too. In the night, sometimes, if she awoke and began to reflect upon all that was going on, she found it was usually to him that her thoughts turned with the greatest pity and compunction.

The 'threadbare old scarecrow of a former lover of Signora Dietrich,' Mrs. Charrington had called him ; and it was a grandly contemptuous way of dismissing the whole subject. But Minna could not dismiss it. A threadbare old scarecrow (human) may suffer, and is not so well able to fight his sufferings or the cause of them as a younger and stronger man might be. She had this conviction very strongly, and would gladly have afforded consolation had it been in her power to do so, but she found no opportunity for it. He avoided her in the house, never came near the studio, and someone said that

Signor Oriole was very much engaged at his office. Minna did not believe it.

It was a wonderful morning, late in April — that wedding-day. As Minna made her way from Casa Dietrich to her studio, a delicious air blew upon her face. The sky was flecked with white clouds. Rain had fallen in the night, and the streets of Rome were glistening with the damp. Now it was dark, now light, under the changing sky. The endless din of the great city resounded on every side, as she walked with a heavy heart through it all. She hoped in a few hours to be many miles away from the city. She took a book and sat in the window waiting till the carriage should come for her which she had ordered on her way hither.

Before the said carriage arrived, she heard a step in the corridor, a subdued knock, and then the door was opened, and Signor Giuseppe presented himself before her. A great weight fell from Minna's heart. She had foreboded she knew not what from his silence and avoidance of her.

'You have come,' she exclaimed with animation, rising and going a little towards him. Then she stopped, silent, not knowing what more to say, he looked so woebegone, so utterly broken, and without heart or courage—so unlike himself.

' I thought you would be at the office,' said Minna gently at last, going up to him and taking his hand.

' So did I,' he replied drearily. ' And to-day, of all days in the year, the poor distraction of my daily drudgery has been taken away from me. Imagine, signora. When I arrived at the office this morning, the porter met me with the announcement that we, the clerks, all had a holiday without any abatement of our week's salary.' He laughed. ' And for what reason, do

you suppose? Because the eldest son of
the head of the firm is to be married this
morning, and is so elated at his good
fortune that he last night got his father to
consent to this arrangement, and each of
us, as we arrived, received the news.
Another wedding,' pursued Signor Giuseppe with melancholy bitterness. ' I suppose the porter thought me mad, for,
instead of smiling and expressing my
delight at the event, I begged to be
allowed to go in and proceed with my
work. "God forbid!" cried the fellow. "Do
you suppose I am going to waste my
precious hours of freedom because you are
fool enough to wish to work when there is
no need of it?" He flourished his keys,
and I came to my senses enough to assure
him that it had only been a joke on my
part. I turned away, and after wandering
about for half an hour, I could bear it
no longer, but came here. I knew you

would not refuse me a corner till the day is over, even——'

'Surely,' said she, ever more and more gently. 'I am thankful you had confidence enough in me to come here. In a few minutes the carriage will come which will take me out of Rome for the day. You will come with me. We will both escape.'

'Go away,' he said unwillingly. 'I had not thought of that.'

'But I think of it. It will be much the best for us both. I am going to Villa Adriana, outside Tivoli. You are just the companion I should wish at that place ; so it is agreed.'

'To Villa Adriana,' he responded, with something like a smile. 'Ah, what a happy afternoon I once spent there with the child and one of her young companions! That is years ago. I will go with you, signora.'

'Yes, of course,' said Minna, speaking much more cheerfully than she felt. She was glad to have gained her end, and had a hope that when they had once set off, and he was within sight of the endless remnants of the former glory of his beloved city, he might cast off some of his present wretchedness, and begin to be interested in the things he had studied so deeply.

It was as she had expected. At first, and for some little time after they had set off, he continued to be sad and silent. Minna could have been the same, but she made an effort, put it aside, and when they at last got into the open country, and into one of the campagna roads, she roused her companion, by asking him what was this or that object which they were passing or approaching. Gradually he also roused, his enthusiasm kindled; he began to relate the history of first one thing and then

another. Then by-and-by, when they had
left behind them every trace of the city,
and were out on the open campagna, they
began to feel its influence—its melancholy grandeur, its solitude, its majesty.
Their driver, who knew his way well, took
them, at Minna's desire, as much out of the
beaten track as possible ; and before they
arrived at the villa they had traversed
roads on which she had never been before.
They were all known, however, to her
companion, who explained them to her,
with their bearing and connection with
other roads, all with the most minute and
perfect exactness.

The clouds gradually grew more white
and less black ; then by degrees unfolded,
spread away and rolled aside, leaving great
expanses of the blue peculiar to those
skies and to no others. The exulting song
of larks was everywhere. Dainty small
flowers of every shape and every hue,

veritable lilies of the field, carpeted the grass at either side of the road. Brilliant little green lizards sunned themselves on large gray stones and fragments of walls and tombs, whose mystery no man should ever unravel. Now and then a flock of sheep in charge of some dark-faced herdsman with a gleaming smile looked up in mild but not alarmed astonishment as they drove by. Turning her head, and looking behind her, Minna saw where the great city lay in the distance, gray or purple or blue, as the clouds shifted and the light flashed or faded ; dim but mighty, with misty-looking domes and cupolas confusedly raising themselves from the general mass, and seeming to beckon back into their charmed circle those who ventured to break forth from it. She had fled from it all this morning, feeling as if one only of the many wickednesses which it sheltered, which were perpetrated within its walls—

the one blot upon its splendour which happened to have come under her own eyes had darkened it for ever to her : but now, despite this feeling which was still there, she felt her heart-strings drawn, as they ever were, by a longing which amounted to pain, as she saw that vague outline in the distance, of the great empress-queen of all cities, past, present, and to come, shrunken from her former dimensions, stripped of her former splendour, modern- ized, vulgarized, patronized (as her companion had once so bitterly complained) by hordes of the curious and pleasure- seeking leisured classes of the world, but matchless still, supreme and imperial still.

She did not speak her thought to Signor Giuseppe. In the present circumstances she was almost ashamed of having such a thought.

They had now left the wilder campagna,

and were within a mile of the villa gates.
They had got into the region of cultivated
fields and trees—into the home of the
almond and olive. The former grew in
orchards showing every shade of blossom,
from a shell-tinted white to the deepest,
richest rose-pink.

The exquisite bloom hung like clouds
over the fields. In the hedges were
masses of blackthorn, like fairy lace flung
over the boughs. Now and then a whiff
of perfume betrayed the near presence of
hidden violets—it was all nearly over, at
the last stage of its loveliness. In another
week it would be too late to see all this
magic of spring. Blossoms would be
shed ; the fairy colours would have given
place to ordinary green leaves. The early
flowers would be over. One might mourn
them, but who could forget that the com-
pensation would be—roses ?

The carriage stopped at the gaudy

modern gate which is the entrance to the
solemnly beautiful cypress avenue, the beginning of the great expanse of ruined
grandeur and desolate beauty which were
once Hadrian's summer palace.

They got out, and arranged with the
driver to meet them at the gates many hours
later. Minna rejoiced his heart by a noble
buona mano for himself and his horses,
bidding him refresh himself and them as
he listed. Then they entered the avenue,
and in ten minutes were wandering, un-
troubled by guides or *custodi*, through those
gardens and passages, past those almost
obliterated ruins and buildings which yet
in their decay and wreck call aloud to
attest the wonder and splendour, beyond
words to describe, of which they once had
formed a part.

The hours flew by while they walked
or sat and ate their lunch, and speculated
and wondered as to the meaning of this,

that, and the other, and Signor Giuseppe
was beguiled into a long, learned, ingenious
dissertation on the character of Hadrian,
which, it will readily be understood, he
had studied with both ardour and acumen ;
and Minna, seated in the deserted
nymphæum, with its falling water, and
melancholy statues, and waving trees,
with a golden sky above, a wilderness
of purple violets below, murmured to herself, 'Aminula, vagula, blandula,' and the
rest of it, and had almost forgotten her
own heartache in pondering on the past,
when suddenly her companion, snatching
his watch from its place, looked at it, and
said, in an indescribable voice :

'Past five. It must be all over and
done with now.'

Minna's heart sank like lead. She felt
a criminal for being here, for having
for one moment felt something that might
be called enjoyment.

'Let us go,' she said abruptly, starting from her place.

*   *   *   *   *

They were well on the homeward way to Rome, and had been almost silent the whole time. Then Minna said casually :

'I will put you down at the door of Casa Dietrich, Signor Oriole. You know that I do not return there.'

'Nor I,' was the curt response. 'You can spare yourself the trouble. I will get out where our ways part.'

'You do not return?' she cried, astonished.

'I ? Never ; if it is intolerable for you, what do you suppose it must be for me ? I told Signora Dietrich some weeks ago, " The day you marry the child to the Australian, I shake the dust of your house from my feet." She laughed at me, and said, " Bené!" Not long before, when I thought, for other reasons, of going away, she almost went on her knees to me to beg me to remain.'

It was the only allusion he had ever made to any words that might have passed between him and Signora Dietrich. Minna knew instinctively that only strong excitement had called it forth.

' But—but——' she stammered, for there came with vivid clearness to her mind the fact that he was exceedingly poor ; had a salary of some seventy or eighty pounds a year, all told, and that but for the home at Casa Dietrich, which, it is true, he paid for with his heart's blood, he must have been reduced to absolute indigence. She felt a chill at her very heart. 'Where do you go, if I may venture to ask ?' she inquired.

' To a little lodging which I have taken. It does not matter where it is,' said he calmly, but with a certain pride at the same time. ' It is no place where I could

ask any of my friends to come and see
me. Do not think I am complaining,'
he went on with perfect self-possession ;
'it is just. I have merited it. My own
weakness, my own selfishness and folly,
taking a shape of which I will not speak
to you, have placed me in the pitiable,
the contemptible position in which you
see me to-day. It is true, I have been
punished already many years for my sin.
It is equally true that no number of years
of expiation could sufficiently atone for
it. I stayed, like you, signora, to the
last moment, in the futile hope that something might happen—to be near her till
the end. Nay, more,' he added, sinking
his voice, 'I called her to me one day
not long ago, and I told her that, if she
chose to confront the risk and the misery
of it, I would go away with her—fly, in
fact, from that house and from her fate,
and would work for her as for my daughter,

would never desert her till life deserted
me. But she would not. She said she
thanked me for what I offered, and trusted
me, but that it would not make things
much better; it would not give her her
mother again. I knew then that this
thing would happen. Of course such
things do happen, and worse, if there can
be any worse. Nothing is too ghastly
to be true. Now I have lost her—it is
merely continuing my life alone.'

' I understand that. But you must not
cut yourself off from everyone and everything,' she said in distress. ' If you will
not tell me where you are going—but, yes,
you will tell me where you are going. I
will never intrude upon you, never interfere with you, but I must know where
you are. Give me your address. I'll
promise not even to look at it unless
there is some urgent reason for my
doing so.'

' I cannot understand why you should hold so much to it,' he remarked ; ' but if it is so you shall have it—I will send it to you. And sometimes, if you will let me, I will come and see you.'

' Indeed you will, or I shall be very unhappy,' she said, almost choked with tears. ' I do not like this. I do not approve of it. I don't know what to do. You have taken me utterly by surprise.'

' Ma che !' he exclaimed, with a shrug of the shoulders. ' Never mind me. Here I will get out,' he added, stopping the coachman at the entrance to a narrow street in the purlieus of Trajan's Forum. ' I will send you the address,' he went on, 'and do not be disturbed if it should be some little time before you see me again. I have need of solitude, to get accustomed to the new order of things.'

He stood beside the carriage, shutting

the door, clasped her hand for a moment, baring his head, and bowing over it with an old-fashioned courtliness which all his troubles had not untaught him.

' Grazie infinite,' he said, resolutely smiling at her and signing to the driver to go on.

Minna had a final glimpse of him standing with his hat in his hand under a street-lamp—for it was now quite dark —and looking after her.

' It is all wrong,' she said to herself —' wrong from beginning to end. What will be the end of it all ?'

CHAPTER XIII.

Two or three weeks passed in a vacant, empty kind of way, and during those weeks Minna was almost alone. She saw Mrs. Charrington two or three times, and that lady condescended to approve of her new apartment, and of her departure from Casa Dietrich. She was even generous enough not to say how very glad she was that 'the girl' was married, and no longer on the spot to disturb her dear Minna's peace of mind, and keep her entangled with 'that set.' She did not say it, but Minna knew very well that she felt it, and smiled to herself rather grimly.

For some little time she did not fret,

either, at Signor Oriole's silence and non-
appearance at the studio. She remembered and understood what he had said
about needing solitude in order to get
accustomed to his new conditions and
mode of life. She presently, however,
began to be sorry that she had let him
slip away from her without giving his
address. He had promised to send it,
but it came not, nor any word from him,
and after two or three weeks had passed
she began to grow uneasy. She remembered the wretched condition of his circumstances and finances when she had last
seen him; his silent unhappiness on parting
with her—an unhappiness through which
at the same time glowed a resolution not
to give up his self-elected solitude ; and
when days had grown into weeks, and still
she heard nothing of him, her alarm began
to increase, and the hopelessness of seeking
through Rome for a man who had chosen

to bury himself in it without leaving any
address became daily more obvious to her.

Once she thought of calling upon Signora Dietrich and asking for news of both
Fulvia and Signor Giuseppe. Then she
laughed aloud all by herself, feeling that
she might as well ask the first person she
met in the street for such information.
Both the girl and the man were unlikely
to confide their affairs to Signora Dietrich,
and even if they should have done so,
Minna felt with what pleasure the signora
would look at her (Mrs. Hastings) should
she be weak enough to go in search of
information—would look at her and send
her about her business rather less wise
than she had been before.

For the first time since she had known
Rome she was weary of it, and longed to
get away from it.   Letters from home also
made her feel that her presence there was
desirable, if not absolutely necessary, to

regulate the affairs of her modest house-
hold, and to set in order feuds amongst
certain old retainers whom the absence of
their mistress had set by the ears. She
wrote home to say that she was coming,
and that all was to be in readiness for her
towards the end of May ; thus she gave
herself still some time to linger and to be
present when Signor Giuseppe came—if
come he should.

Meantime, in order to try to forget her
anxiety, she had been working hard at the
bust of Fulvia, and she intended to take it
home with her, finished. Looking upon it,
she knew that it was beautiful—knew that,
in her own intense feelings for and sympathy with its original, she had succeeded
in throwing into the beautiful sad features
a whole world of meaning—of grace, of
sorrow, of proud endurance. She stopped
sometimes in her work, and gazed upon it,
and pondered on the matter.

What would Fulvia's marriage—her so-called marriage—make of her? It was bound to work some great change or development in her character. Would it ripen her early into a more than usually noble woman, proud and reticent, suffering and strong? Would it crush her into a hopeless slave, terrified and cowering before the tyrant to whom she was tied? Or would it harden her into marble, stiffen all her girlish brightness into a chilly glitter of the conventional, professional cheerfulness all must wear, unless they wish the world to invent the most wonderful calumnies concerning them and their lives? For it is true that the inwardly unhappy, in certain circumstances, must either calumniate themselves or be calumniated by others.

Minna could form no idea on the subject. She would have given a good deal to learn something about it, but no sign came. There was no news—no word of Fulvia, who had disappeared utterly when she had departed with Marchmont for Milan on their way to London.

Minna's state of mind grew more and more anxious, more and more perturbed, as time went on, and the day beyond which her departure must no longer be delayed approached with remorseless rapidity. She was longing to leave Rome —to breathe an air which was not tainted with the horrors and the sins of thousands of years, horrors and sins which had never troubled her till the one horror, the one sin, was perpetrated which went home to her and appealed to her. Now it seemed to her, when she walked abroad, threading the narrow streets, or passing under or beside the awful piles of ruin, as she glanced at the hoary grayness of the Forum, looking ashen and ghastly in the dazzling May sunshine, as she looked upwards at

the grim frown of the overhanging fragments of the Palatine, that the whole place
reeked with sin and crime, and with the
deadly odour of shameful bargains and
sales of human bodies and souls. It was
morbid, she felt, or tried to feel, but it was
very strong and very real ; and, returning
one Friday evening from the comparative
cool of Doria Pamfili gardens, into the
odours and the noises of the teeming
streets below, she was suddenly seized
with a wild, unreasoning craving after a
breath of the air, fresh from the moor, salt
from the sea, which she knew was blowing
round her old gray house far in the North,
at home. The everlasting glare of blue
and gold in the sky and sun oppressed
her ; the voluptuous languor of the nights,
loud with music and vocal with thrilling
notes of song, made her feverish and restless. Had she followed her own impulse,
she would have fled within a few hours,

nor ever rested till the Alps were between her and this great insolent sorceress city.

She could not fly. Business still tied her for a few days, and the idea that there was someone somewhere within those mazes of streets with whom she had clasped hands in friendship, and whose misery was to her nervous unrest as the ocean compared to a fretting brooklet, was a torment to her.

Still time flew by relentlessly. It wanted now only two days to the date fixed for her departure. She had been at the studio all one afternoon, superintending the packing of the bust of Fulvia, which, heavy though it was, she had determined to take with her own personal luggage, and also that of the as yet unfinished statue, which, packed and enveloped with the greatest care, was to go by sea to Liverpool, and thence to be despatched to her home. The carriers were to come to-morrow for the great package. She intended to return herself, see it off the premises, and pack up and put away the things she was leaving here, for she intended to retain the rooms for at least a year, against her possible return to Rome. The noise and the bustle were over. The men, satisfied with the *buona mano* they had received, grinned from ear to ear, wished her a successful journey and said a cordial *a rivederci*. They clattered down the stairs and away, and when the last noise of their feet had died away, she got up and looked rather sorrowfully round the shabby room, now quite turned upside down, in which she had spent so many happy hours, and so many sad ones too. It was useless to linger. The place now sent a shudder through her. She would go away, to her lodging, and busy herself in beginning the packing necessary for her journey.

It was a hot May evening, towards six o'clock. She put on her broad straw hat, took her gloves and sunshade from the table, and left the room, locking the door behind her. Slowly she descended the cool dark staircase, and went through the court, deep in shadow, towards the dazzling white light in the street. As she slowly paced along, her eye was caught by another shadow which flitted along, close to the wall—and crowning the shadow was a man's white face. Some little thrill, some intuitive knowledge, darted through her veins and heart. She stopped suddenly and decidedly, arrested the shadow, and laid her hand upon its arm.

'Signor Oriole—at last! Why have you treated me in this way?'

'Why have I treated myself in this way, you should rather ask,' he said; 'do you suppose that if I had had anything good to tell you I should not have been with

you before now ? My news was always
bad ; therefore, though I have many times
been as far as this court, I have never
mounted the stair.'

'Bad news —of Fulvia?' she added, still
instinctively holding him fast by the arm
lest he should yet escape.

'No, of myself,' said he, with some
naïveté, 'though, of course, it would not
matter about me if she were not concerned in it too.'

'Come upstairs,' said Minna decidedly,
as she turned back. 'Come upstairs, and
tell me everything about it.'

He made no resistance, but suffered her
to lead him upstairs. She unlocked the
door, and they at once stood within the
dreary, half-dismantled room. Closing the
door behind them, she looked at him.
She did not ask him how he did. There
was no need for that. He was not at
all well, as anyone could see. Signor

Giuseppe was a broken man. The signs of that condition are well known, and easily to be recognised. They do not need to be recapitulated here.

'Sit down,' said Minna gently, 'and tell me what has happened to you, and why you have never come to see me.'

'I have had a great misfortune,' said Signor Giuseppe. 'I have come into a fortune—not a large one, but enough, if it had come in time, to——'

He stopped abruptly. Minna, breathless, wondered if his troubles had really affected his mind. But there was no appearance about him of a disordered brain, only of a profoundly sad heart.

'Tell me about it,' she said.

'Of course I should have come to see you before if this had not happened,' he said. 'It was very soon after I last saw you; in fact, only two or three days after. One day at the office I found some papers

for me, which had been sent to one or two
wrong addresses. I ought to have had
them a week before—mark you, a week!'
he said in a louder voice, raising his hand
and gesticulating a little. 'I have told
you, and you know all about it, that once
I was different. I was not what I am
now. I was a gentleman. I was not this
broken-down old vagabond whom you
have always known, and to whom you
have still been kind. When I gave up
my own estate, which was sufficient,
though not large, and left my country, I
left also others behind me—relations, connections. Amongst them, an uncle, my
father's brother, who was rather a singular
old character. I will not trouble you with
an account of him. He was an eccentric.
He was a bachelor, something also of a
miser, and very much of a curmudgeon.
He lived alone on his property, and we
saw little or nothing of him. When I

went to say good-bye to him, and to tell
him that I was going to fight for the
freedom of my country, and for her unity,
and that I was disposing of my property
in order to be able the more effectually to
help, he said : "Beppino mio, you are a
complete and utter fool. Fight for your
country as much as you please—young
blood must have an outlet, and that is at
least a respectable style of sowing your
wild oats ; but keep a whole suit of clothes
in which to dress yourself when the battle
is over, a chimney nook in which to rest
and warm yourself, a fowl for the pot, a
vine wherefrom to fill the vats, and a field
of corn from which to provide bread for
yourself. Otherwise you will find that, by
the time your country is free, you yourself
are a slave. You have never been accustomed to work for your livelihood.
Take my word for it, your plan will not
answer." I was then twenty-two. I paid

no heed to his words, but went my own
way. You know the rest. Two months
ago, I believe, I would have welcomed
back the Austrians if I could have been
secure of fifty thousand lire. But I might
as well have cried for the moon. And
yet, nearly a week before the child was
married, far more than fifty thousand lire
were mine, had I known it. He died, it
seems, months ago, at his property far
away in the country, in Sicily. He was
ninety-five. Only think, signora, of anyone being unlucky enough to live to be
ninety-five! I was his only living direct
relative. All the others were gone.
Everything that he had comes to me. I
am again in the possession of an income
—nay, I am well off, at ease, so far as my
ideas go . . . and I did not know it in
time to save her.'

There was a long silence. Sweeping
over Minna's mind came the full sense of

the miserable, sordid tragedy of the situation. Another thought, which she would
not for the world have hurt him by utter-
ing, was that his poor little property would
not have had a feather's weight in the
balance with Signora Dietrich when she
was arranging Fulvia's marriage with
Marchmont.

'What can I say?' she said at last.
'There is nothing to say.'

'Nothing. I quite agree with you,' he
replied bitterly, and they were both silent
again, till at last she asked:

'And your work—and your lodging?
What are you doing about that?'

'As for the lodging, it is not worth
while to change it,' he said despondently.
'I am in the same place—Via——'

He named a wretched little street, quite
near to where he had left her on that
evening when they had been to Hadrian's
Villa, near the Forum of Trajan, and

Minna felt all the sordid wretchedness and discomfort which he had gone through pierce her own heart.

' But you go to the office every day ?' she inquired gently.

' No more,' he said.   ' They did not want me.   I had begun to make mistakes. They were very kind, but they wanted to get rid of me.'

Then he told her a story between the lines of which she was easily able to read. He had evidently clung to his post at the office with a pitiable tenacity : it was some-thing for him to do ; it was a remnant of the old accustomed order of things ; in so far, it was a consolation, and it kept him going.   He had been many years with that particular firm of lawyers.   The prin-cipal was a kind-hearted man, and had always treated him well, and when, within the last month or two, it was found that Oriole's work was always going wrong,

was full of mistakes, and that he constantly forgot the commissions or pieces of
writing entrusted to him, Signor Gismondi
began to make inquiries. He wished to
be kind and considerate, but business had
to be thought of. The result of the
inquiries discovered to him that Oriole
had come into some property, which
placed him in an independent if very
modest position, and above want. There
was then no need for further scruples.
Signor Gismondi sent for his gray-headed
clerk, and, as kindly as he could, intimated
to him that his services were to be dis-
pensed with—a new and a younger man
was to be engaged in his place—after
Easter, when he pleased—*ecco !*

A last rag of pride and sensitiveness
sent a red flush into Signor Giuseppe's
cheek. With a bow, the majesty of which
good Signor Gismondi could not have
attained to, had he practised for twenty

years, Oriole intimated that it was just the
same to him when he left—to day, to-
morrow, next week. If they had not
already engaged the services of someone
else, he was willing to wait just to accommo-
date them, as long as they liked. Signor
Gismondi seized eagerly upon this opening for softening the blow, and assured
Giuseppe that he would confer a very
great favour upon them by remaining for
another week, until they had looked about
them for a person suitable to replace him.
Agreed! Signor Giuseppe was in much
better spirits that week, being under the
impression that he was really doing a
favour to the firm of Gismondi e Nipoti.
But when the week was over and the
occupation gone, oh! then was Signor
Giuseppe to be pitied. Well for them
who, reduced to such a condition of drift-
ing loneliness, have one compassionate eye
fixed upon them—only one! They may

be saved. It is such as he, reduced perhaps a stage lower in grief and hopelessness, who, looking round instinctively in a
last effort to find something which shall
encourage them to remain in the world,
and failing to do so, meeting no out-
stretched hand, seeing no eye which has
any attention in it for them—such as these
it is who, lingering near the river, some
evening or other plunge into it, or who
purchase their dose of poison, and, after
keeping it for a time, suddenly swallow it,
or discharge the pistol which has been
long loaded and ready, or who infallibly
find some gate or other open, through
which they can creep out of one blackness
into another that is yet darker.

Signor Giuseppe had not got as far as
that, though he was well on the way to it.
Minna, looking at him, understood it all;
and an immense pity, an immense longing
to help and save, came over her. There

was a silence as they sat facing one
another in the room, which was now very
quiet. A ray of warm, rather stuffy sunshine had crept round to the window, and
mercilessly lighted up all the rather shabby,
threadbare details of the place. It left
Minna in the shade, but fell upon her
companion, and showed her the profound
sadness and hopelessness of his expression.
He had aged by twenty years. The man
who, when she had first seen him, had
struck her as barely beginning to be
elderly, was now old. If no one helped
him he would be lost. That was what she
felt with a strength of pity and of conviction which swamped all other feelings.
She broke the silence rather abruptly.

' Do you see what a state of disorder
the room is in ?' she asked.

' I thought there was something different
about it,' he replied, looking round. ' Are
you going to make some alterations ?'

'Oh no ; I am only going to shut it up.
I am leaving Rome the day after to-
morrow,' she replied, with studied careless-
ness.

Her announcement had exactly the effect
she had calculated upon.

'Leaving Rome!' he echoed, with a
great start and look of blank dismay ; and
then, naïvely enough :

'What is to become of me ?'

'Oh, that is easily settled. I am going
straight home to England—to my own
house. You must come with me.'

'Impossible,' ejaculated Signor Giuseppe,
springing from his chair and looking very
much agitated. 'Signora, you speak with
all the calm, deliberate frenzy peculiar to
your nation. But you should not mock at
my misfortunes.'

'I never was less inclined to mock in
my life,' said Minna, settling herself into
the corner of the sofa, prepared to do

battle for any length of time. 'What I
propose is the utmost common-sense, and
is also the only thing to be done. To-
night you go home and arrange your plans
for getting ready to-morrow. To-morrow
you employ in getting all that you want for
the journey, and for a prolonged stay in
our bleak country during its so-called
summer. You must spend some of this
money that you have got,' she went on
with the utmost tranquillity, trying hard
not to smile at the almost paralyzed
astonishment with which he continued to
regard her. 'It will be all right. The
day afterwards you will be quite ready,
with your luggage, and I shall call
for you in good time'—with emphasis—'on
my way to the station. Three-forty is the
time of the train. Don't forget. We
shall go to Milan, and rest there, and then
pursue our way to England. I will write
to-night to my housekeeper to say I am

bringing someone with me, and that she is
to have a room ready. There is really no
more to be said.'

' But there is—a great deal,' burst out
Signor Giuseppe. ' And it may all be expressed in one word : Impossible !'

Minna smiled. The argument was a
long one. She had to fight the objections
and doubts and unwillingness of a man
whose last experiences of life, outside his
own city, had been the rough and painful
ones of a soldier, subject to all kinds of
pain and privations ; one who had come
into the great city after endless and
exhausting struggles, and who clung to
it as one who felt that he had a nook
there which he knew, whereas all the world
outside was cold and strange and empty.
If one must die, it were better to die at
home.

He realized, with an intensity which
showed what strength and life still lay

behind the broken-down outer man, that he was a wreck and a ruin ; he was sure he would be a hateful burden, a nuisance— a nuisance to anyone whose companion he might be.   Minna was very patient.   Point by point she fought his doubts and fears and scruples, and at last told him that, whatever he might think, he had still duties in the world, and that he ought to go where he could gain strength and prepare himself to meet them.

' And my duties, signora, what may they be ?   Where do they lie ?'

' As long as Fulvia lives you have a duty to her,' replied Minna calmly, and she saw him start and turn pale.   ' You cannot cast it aside.   One day you will meet her again.   I am absolutely certain of it.   You do not know in what condition you may meet her.   You do not know what her need may be, nor how you can minister to it, but this much is certain :

that you ought to be ready to help her
if she should need help—and how should
she not need it, sooner or later ?'

It was this argument which, more than
any of the others, prevailed. When he
went away, she had his promise, and she
had made him give her his exact address.
He also promised to see her on the
morrow, and let her know that he was
getting ready to go with her. He had
even come so far back to the real, practical
world as to wonder, with ill-concealed
uneasiness, what her friends and relations
would say to her importation into their midst
of such a wretched scarecrow as himself.

'Fortunately,' said Minna, 'I am not
dependent on what my friends and relations say. And they are not barbarians,
either.'

He did not fail her. He was ready and
waiting when she called for him at the
appointed time—a transformed man, as

to outward appearance, though with a somewhat nervous and scared expression, as if no such step had ever been taken by anyone before.

The noise and bustle of the station and the departure of the train were over. They were outside the city. The long uninteresting line of the gigantic basilica of San Paolo without the Walls had gradually disappeared from their view. The campagna stretched desolately around them. The sun went down in the west, in a red ball of fire. Signor Oriole's eyes strained into the distance, towards the faint-blue cloud which still showed him where the city lay, and his lips moved as he murmured to himself :

' Rome—for whom I have lived—grant me to die in thine arms !'

CHAPTER XIV.

MAY in London, five years later. The weather was bad, and everyone said the season was a dull one. To Minna Hastings it did not much matter whether it was dull or bright. She had come to spend a fortnight in town with some friends; she had never been very fond of London. She had quitted her home with regret, and though not exactly longing to be back there, she was yet quite ready to return to it when the time should come for her to do so. This was, perhaps, ungrateful on her part, for there was no doubt that this year Minna had one morning wakened to find herself, in a small way, and amongst a certain set, famous.

The figure of the workman, which for three years had been standing finished in her studio at home, had been sent to one of the London galleries, accepted, well placed, and seen of all who visited that gallery. To Minna's own surprise, it had proved an immense 'take.' Critics, alike with those who were not critics, had been fascinated with it. It had been reviewed, admired, talked about, till Minna was rather sorry she had sent it. It represented so much more to her than it ever could to those who saw it. Its strength and grace were praised — its originality, its boldness, its daring simplicity, and so forth. The most curious things were said about it. The artist, when she met with these lucubrations, rubbed her eyes, sometimes in vexation, sometimes in amusement, at the intentions which were attributed to her.

' Mrs. Hastings has evidently,' said one oracle, 'made a profound study of the finest models of modern French sculpture, and the intention she seeks to convey in this masterly work is obvious.'

So obvious that, as obvious things often do, it escaped the knowledge of its author, who only said to herself, ' Thank heaven they do not know the history of all that I put into it !'

Then came applications from sundry would-be buyers, known and unknown. Many hundreds of pounds might have been Minna's had she been disposed to part with her work. But she could not do so. Feeling forbade it, and, luckily for her, circumstances allowed her to keep it.

She never had forgotten, never could forget, what had passed between her and Signor Giuseppe that evening when she had shown it to him, and had heard what

he had to say about it—and about some
other things.

She was persuaded with difficulty by
her friends to go and look at it one
morning.   She knew not what shock came
over her as her eyes encountered the
figure of her own handiwork, to the
finishing of which had gone so many
thoughts, wishes, and aspirations.   There
he stood, confronting her as she placed herself before him, seeming to live and stand
out from all the surrounding things.   She
met his patient, steady eyes, which asked
her, ' Do you know me in all this foreign
crowd, so alien to me and to you ?   Do you
not remember those still hours of solitude
and striving in which you lived with me
and made me what I am ?   When will you
take me back to be with you again, since
neither of us can be where we would—at
home in Rome ?'   A choking came in her
throat as she thought of the shabby old

studio—the hours of intense life, both of joy and of sorrow, and she turned abruptly away, while her friends walked round the figure, and exclaimed, and admired, and put the wonted questions to her, ' Minna, how did you come to think of it ? What put it into your head ?' ' I could never have thought of such a thing if I had been crowned for it,' and so on.

When the slight mist which covered her eyes had cleared from them, and she could see clearly again, she took time to look round, and found herself in a kind of little *tribuna*, round which, in an inner circle, as it were, were disposed statues and busts, while on the walls hung pictures. She glanced round, and began to examine the latter ; she found herself almost in front of one which soon arrested her attention. It represented a corner of the great church of Santa Maria-sopra-Minerva at Rome, and one of the little episodes which one con-

stantly sees occurring in Roman churches—
one half of the episode, at least, is common
enough. A young girl, accompanied by a
servant, drops an alms into the hand of a
beggar. The beggar is an old woman,
whose withered countenance lights up as
she glances into the face of the girl. Just
behind the old woman is the figure of a
young man, whose eyes are fixed with
a passion of admiration and entreaty upon
the girl's face, which, sweet and calm and
cold, smiles upon the old woman, and does
not even see him. No possibility of mis-
taking the meaning in those eyes, nor the
prayer for notice and love in the entire
attitude and look. There was an emotional
quality in this picture which went far to
triumph over a good many faults of colour
and execution.

As Minna looked at it, a strange feeling
stole over her. The faces of the young
man and the girl were not portraits, but

there was in them a haunting likeness to
two faces she had known, which likeness
sent a thrill through her. Hastily turning
over the leaves of her catalogue, she found
the number and title of the picture, and
a scarcely suppressed ' Ah !' broke from her
lips.

' The Two Mendicants — Hans Riemann.'

Fastened to the spot, she examined the
picture with eager attention. Never had
she imagined her cousin Hans to be possessed of such subtlety in expressing a
graceful thought. It was he—it was
Fulvia ; not boldly and openly portrayed,
but hinted at, indicated, shadowed forth,
as it were. Patent to her, who was familiar
with them both, and with their stories—a
veiled mystery, not even a mystery—
merely a delicate attractive picture to any
outsider who knew nothing of the drama
which underlay it all.

'I knew it—I was certain of it!' Minna said to herself, but quite beneath her breath. 'I taxed him with it, and he turned it off. Why did he not speak out at the time? Oh, I would have helped him through everything. I would have become poor that he might have succeeded. If Fulvia had had a lover—one whom she loved, at that time—she might have been saved. She would have had a strength to resist which would have carried her through everything. . . . Hans, you fool! And how he has improved! I used to think his things rather finikin, I didn't care for them—but this shows a perfectly enormous advance.'

'What are you looking at?' asked the loud, cheerful voice of one her friends, just at her elbow. 'That! Oh, isn't it odd that Mr. Riemann's picture should have got put close to your piece of sculpture? It's a pretty thing, very. Do you

know, I said the other day that, according
to the accepted rule in such things, and
judging from the outside only, the picture
ought to have been by the woman, and
the statue by the man. The picture is
so delicate, you know, and refined and
emotional, and all that. (I hear he has
sold it very well.) And the statue—well,
you know, Minna, it has been praised for
its brutality : in the French sense of the
word, not the English.'

To all of which Minna made little re-
joinder, except a faint smile. She did
manage to murmur that the picture was
very charming, and that Hans had made
great progress during the last few years.

Then they moved on, laughing at Minna
for not being more interested in the public
view of her own work. They made the
weary round of the gallery, and looked at
all the most talked-of pictures, and at last
went away to get lunch somewhere, and

then to go and see some other show. All
day long there dwelt in Minna's mind the
tender grace of that painting. She wondered who had bought it. She was longing to possess it herself. She felt un-
reasonably annoyed and vexed with the
happy owner, whoever he or she might be.
And when at night, wearied in brain and
body with the empty whirl of the day, she
placed her head upon her pillow, the
scene again rose before her eyes : ' The
Two Mendicants '—the gracious figure,
whose hand was relieving the one, and
passing by the other, not even seeing him.
Minna said within herself, ' I'll go again.
I shall go and look at it as often as I
can escape from them and get there
alone.'

Her last thought was, ' Shall I tell
Beppo ? I think not. He never speaks
about it now, but I am sure the pain of
that time has never been less in his soul

than it was just when it happened. It
would hurt him. No; I won't say anything.'

She carried out her intention, and, under
one pretext or another, managed several
times to escape from her companions, slip
alone into the gallery, thread her way
through its rooms, and finally, with a sigh
of pleasure and pain combined, seat herself
before the picture, with her back to the
statue, while she looked, wondered, and
speculated.

Where was Fulvia? What had become
of her? What had she grown into? Not
one word had been heard of her since her
marriage. She had never written to anyone at home—neither to her mother, nor to
Giuseppe, nor to Minna herself. At the
time of the marriage it had been Marchmont's intention to take his bride first to
London and Paris, and sooner or later to
Australia, to 'show' her, in his own charac-

teristic language, to his 'people' there, who were understood to be very rich, and given to admire sumptuous and beautiful things—such things as Fulvia would have every chance of becoming.

Whether he had carried out this programme Minna had never heard. She thought it probable ; she thought it even possible that he might have settled in Australia, having discovered that he was a bigger man in Sydney or Melbourne than he would be in London or Paris. Of one thing only she was certain—that they had never revisited Rome.

On this particular morning Minna was at her post before the picture, and passing through her mind was the wonder where Hans could now be. The easy-going young fellow whom she had known in Rome at Casa Dietrich had made some way in the world as an artist, but chiefly as a painter of what seemed to Minna 'prettiness.' Even in this case she would have mistrusted her own judgment and thought her delight in the picture to be more the result of the associations it had for her mind than its own inherent merit, but the verdict on all sides was to the same effect as her own.

In a half-dream she sat, leaning back in the comfortable settee, and vaguely hearing the voices and footsteps of those who passed, but not heeding them, unless they stood before her and actually interrupted her view of the picture.

Voices behind her of two women—probably young women.

'Oh, Ethel, this must be the statue that Tom was talking about. He said it was splendid. What is it called?'

Leaves of a catalogue were fluttered quickly over—then, in dulcet tones :

'"In the sweat of thy brow. Roma, 18——" What on earth does it mean?'

'A horrid, common working man, and nothing else. Well, I cannot understand what anyone can see to admire in that, I must say. Let's see—artist's name, Minna Hastings. A woman! Just fancy any lady deliberately setting to work and carving out the figure of a dirty half-naked man like that! What a queer creature she must be!'

Minna was interested, charmed. She did not move, but gazed steadily before her at the picture. Now the two speakers were immediately behind her. There was no crowd, and they could quite well see over her head.

'Now just look what different things strike different people!' said the more decided voice of the two. 'Look at that picture—"The Two Mendicants." I call it lovely. Isn't that girl sweet? And the old woman—splendid! And the young man. Ethel'— in an excited whisper—'he

really has a look of—don't you know?
Those long eyes and that intense look—
what Fräulein would call *schwärmerisch*.
I do like it. Well, you see, that's Rome,
too. " In the church of Santa Maria-
sopra-Minerva, Roma." And the painter
is a man—Hans Riemann, you see. Well,
all one can say is that some men have
much nicer tastes than some women. . . .
Hadn't we better go on to the next room,
or we shall not get it all done before lunch?'
'Oh yes! Come!'
They walked away. Minna, half turning
her head, stole a look after them. A
couple of fresh-looking, 'nicely'-dressed,
rather meaningless English girls. There
are hundreds and thousands of them, gaily
passing their opinions on everything that
comes under their notice in the heavens
above or in the earth beneath. Minna
smiled to herself, and again became lost in
contemplation of the picture.

The door into the small room in which she sat was behind her. For some time she was left in undisturbed solitude. Then there were footsteps behind her, of two persons. She paid no heed to them. They stopped—evidently in front of her work. There was a prolonged silence, till at last a man's voice said, earnestly and softly :

'Well, is it not what I told you ? Did I do right to bring you ?'

A woman's voice in reply, which yet sounded almost as if the speaker spoke to herself, in a half-dream.

'Yes ; it is the same—Roma. Oh, I am very glad you brought me !'

She spoke Italian. For one moment Minna's heart sprang with such a wild throb to her throat that she could neither move nor speak. Then it seemed to stop altogether ; then went beating on again at five times its usual pace. It all took but

a couple of seconds. She had recovered
her power of speech and motion. She
rose swiftly from her place, and turned
towards the speakers, her face in a pale
blaze of emotion.

It was true. There was no deception.
That was Hans, older, handsomer, with
his boyish tendency to lounge developed
into the supple ease of a man of the world,
but with—the words of the young lady who
had been so pleased with his picture came
into Minna's mind almost grotesquely :
' Those long eyes and that intense look '—
the eyes and the look which are so difficult
to read aright in man or woman —
experience only can prove whether they
mean a character weak, selfish, and
sensuous, or earnest and passionately
clinging in its loves and hates, hopes
and fears. Whatsoever the look might
betoken, the man was Hans ; and that
woman beside him, in the full splendour

of youth and beauty, in the full pomp of
the costliest simplicity of dress, with the
bearing of a queen, and the utterly calm
and self-possessed, rather cool aspect—that
was Fulvia.

For a moment the three stood looking
at each other, while their expressions
changed half a dozen times. It was Minna
who spoke first, in a voice which she could
not force to be steady, tried she never so
hard.

' Fulvia !' she said.   ' Hans !'

' Minna, by Jove!' ejaculated Hans,
recovering from his astonishment. ' I
never was more floored in my life, though
why I should have been I'm sure I don't
know.   It's the most natural thing in the
world for you to be here—just as it is for
us.   I have brought Mrs. Marchmont, you
see, to show her an old acquaintance.'   He
smiled and looked at Minna's statue.

A great change had come over Fulvia's

face.   She had grown very pale ; her
steady eyes wavered—one could almost
have sworn that, for one moment, they
were dim.   While Hans was talking, she
and Minna had clasped hands and were
looking at one another.   Minna was far
past speaking.   It was as if her own
beloved child, long lost, had returned to
her.   Fulvia also seemed not to be
possessed of much eloquence.   A grave,
sweet smile dawned upon her lips ; in a
low voice and with an accent of indescribable tenderness she said :

' Signora carissima !'

It was the exact tone in which she had
often spoken to Minna, when she had sat
with her five years ago, in her little salon
at Casa Dietrich, discussing the woeful
future.   As she spoke, with a swift, graceful gesture she lifted Minna's hands to
her lips, and kissed them, one after the
other.

The elder woman was shaken to her innermost being. She felt that, if she spoke, tears would rush from her eyes and choke her voice. After a long time, 'At last!' she stammered out, and, unable to bear it any longer, she sat down hastily on the bench, and, still holding Fulvia's hand, drew her to the space beside her.

'Sometimes,' she said, recovering breath, 'the gods are good. Sometimes they send us what we want. They have been good to me to-day.'

'Whether they have been good to me, I can hardly yet decide,' said Hans in a melancholy voice. He was practically left out in the cold while this interview was going on. 'Anyhow,' he continued, 'they have blessed me with sense enough to see that I had better retire while I can do so with self-respect, and leave you two to your conversation. But you will

perhaps favour me with the merest indica-
tion as to what I am to do for you later.
Shall I disappear altogether, and return
no more? Shall I come back for you,
Mrs. Marchmont, and take you home?
Or, in short, I am at your orders, ladies,
when once I know what those orders
are.'

'Poor Hans!' said Minna, smiling, and
looking at him more attentively. She
was struck again with his altered appearance. She had not seen him now
for more than three years, and had heard
very little about him. He was, as she
knew, about eight-and-twenty, but he
looked considerably older. In some
aspects he looked like eight-and-thirty.
He had a dark, bronzed, richly-coloured
face, grave, soft, dark-brown eyes, and
a brown, pointed beard and moustache.
The general aspect of his face was one of
gravity—gravity, dignity, and poetical,

artistic beauty. There was nothing left of his old, boyish manner, except its simplicity, for he had the great charm of simplicity.

All this Minna realized and saw, as, with one of her hands laid upon one of Fulvia's, she looked up at him, and listened to what he said. She turned to Fulvia.

'What do you wish, Fulvia? What can you do for me? I mean, how long can we be together? And is this the best place? I can take you to my room at my friends' if you like, where we can be alone.'

'I think this is as good a place as any,' said Fulvia, who now spoke English, with but little foreign intonation. 'We can then arrange how to meet again. You are very kind, Mr. Riemann. I don't think there is anything you can do for me. I ordered my carriage to be here at one.

It can come, and wait, or Mrs. Hastings
and I can leave whenever we like. I
shall see you again to-night, I suppose?
Good-morning.'

With a gracious bow of her head she
dismissed him. Minna called after him.

'Hans, you will come and see me. I'm
staying at the Montons', where you have
been many a time. I shall be there
about a week longer. Send me a line,
and I will be at home when you come.'

'Very well,' said he, without the faintest
trace of ungraciousness—definable, at any
rate. For all the suavity of his manner,
Minna knew that he was annoyed at the
meeting. She, however, cared nothing
for that. She smiled upon him. He
lifted his hat, and saying 'A rivederci'
went slowly out of the room.

'Now, Fulvia, tell me something about
yourself,' said Minna, looking at her companion and stroking her hand.

CHAPTER XV.

'CARA SIGNORA,' said Fulvia, with a slight smile, 'I have literally nothing to tell you about myself. I saw you five years ago. I was almost seventeen then. It is therefore obvious that I am now nearly twenty-two. Since that day I have travelled a great deal, seen a great deal, and learnt a great deal. That was to be expected. A child of seventeen must necessarily be densely ignorant of everything outside the schoolroom and the nursery. But a child with any intelligence must necessarily learn a great deal in so long a time as has passed since we met, and I have had ample opportunities for learning—oh, ample.'

She broke off, smiling—a sweet, frigid
smile. Minna scarcely heeded its sweetness but felt all its frigidity, which com-
municated itself to her own heart.

'You have never been to Rome again,
I suppose?' she asked quickly, and this
time Fulvia's face grew hard, though she
still smiled.

'Not to Rome. We have been, I think,
almost everywhere else, and, as you per-
ceive, are now in London.'

'Living here, or for the season?' asked
Minna.

'Neither one nor the other. We are in
a kind of transition period. We came
here from the South of France, where we
spent nearly the whole winter. I hate the
Riviera—don't you? There is such a
spasmodic attempt at gaiety and amusing
yourself there, which comes to nothing,
however hard you may try. To an active-
minded person like myself, it is a frightful

life, but there is an institution at ——
where cases like my husband's could be
treated, so we stayed there.'

' Cases like your husband's—is he ill ?'

' Yes, he is ill.'

' Is it anything serious ?   Did he benefit
by the treatment you speak of ?'

' Not in the least, so far as I can see.
This illness began, about eighteen months
ago, with partial paralysis.   It has continued to be partial paralysis ever since,
and it is partial paralysis now.   All the
baths and waters (we have tried those too)
and massage and electricity in the world
will never produce the least effect upon it,
but of course, when people are ill, they
like to try everything, and my theory is
to indulge them in their wish.   It gives
them something to do and think of, at any
rate.'

She smiled, and adjusted the flowers in
the belt of her white gown.

'Then you have come to London for further treatment?'

'For further advice. The doctors at Cannes told us the specialists whom we ought to consult here, so we have obediently come, and consulted them. Of course they don't tell him—nor even me—but they know perfectly well what it is. It will not kill him yet—at least, it is not likely to do so. If he were a poor man, and unable to get proper attention, he might die very soon. But he is a rich man, who can command everything that he wants, and he may live for—a—great—many—years,' said Fulvia, in quiet, clear tones, with little pauses between the words, as she reached the end of her sentence. 'It may get worse. He might die of something quite different; or he might have a stroke, and die of it; but he will never be better. It is a very unpleasant thing for him, but, as one of the doctors told him a little while ago, it is the result entirely of the life he chose to live as a young man. It was quite too hard a life for his constitution, and he may be thankful that it is not something much more horrible.'

Minna was silent, feeling a horror in her heart. Fulvia sat beside her, with her little firm, delicately gloved hands folded lightly on her knee. Her face was like the face of Fulvia Dietrich, with startling yet indefinable differences. The girlish indecision of outline had entirely disappeared, and left an exquisitely modelled face, with firm, statuesque curves of cheek and lip, pure aquiline line of nose, and a broad, rather low forehead—that is, a forehead on which the hair grew low, the same thick, glistening hair which the girl Fulvia had had. The slim figure of the young maiden had bloomed out into the full strength and magnificent outlines of early womanhood. She had grown taller, Minna was convinced, as well as having taken on this perfect outline with its larger, firmer curves and commanding beauty. The expression on Fulvia's face was one of the utmost calm and placidity. Did she, or did she not, feel anything ? Minna speculated. In speaking of her husband, not a ray of feeling of any kind had betrayed itself. Whether she were glad or sorry, bored, disgusted, satisfied, it would have been utterly impossible to tell. Minna maintained an anxious, uneasy silence. Presently Fulvia resumed :

' Of course, under these circumstances it is ridiculous to talk of being here " for the season." He cannot go out at all, and I certainly cannot, alone, in London. We are in lodgings—a hotel was too noisy for him. The doctors recommend him to go to the country. They have told him this much : that he will never be strong again,

and must never dream of making any
exertions to speak of; and they talk about
country air and a quiet life'—-she laughed,
for the first time during their meeting, a
little cold laugh of mingled amusement
and contempt. 'So he is debating whether
to buy a place, or hire a place in the
country—and where. That is really all
that keeps us in London now. I have
already taken several most tiresome rail-
way journeys, to see different places which
were to let or sell—nothing suitable, of
course, when I got there. And I am sure
I don't know when or if anything will
ever be settled.'

'How I wish you would come into
our neighbourhood! There is a place
close to mine,' exclaimed Minna impul-
sively, 'or rather, I ought to say, I occupy
a sort of "at his gates" position with
regard to it. It is the great house of
the neighbourhood, and mine is only

a little old-fashioned place.   But it is
to let or sell at this present moment,
and nobody has taken it yet.'

' Where do you live ?' asked Fulvia.

' Up in the North—at West Wall, in
Durham.   It is near the sea, and it is
near the moors, so that if healthiness
is any consideration I am sure we can
offer it to you.'

' How cold!' exclaimed Fulvia, with
a little shiver.

' Ah, yes, you child of the South !   It
is cold, it is gray, and it is bleak—towards
the sea, at any rate.   But we have warm
hearts, and the Hall is built in a sheltered
spot.'

' Who are " we " ?' asked Fulvia
tranquilly, and not repelling the sugges-
tion which Minna had made.

' We are '— she paused abruptly, then
went on quickly : 'you will be surprised,
if you have heard no home news—Signor

Oriole lives with me now. "We" are
Signor Oriole and myself, and Rhoda
Hamilton, my niece.   She is nearly
always with me.   She is my brother's
only child, and he is a widower.'

'Signor Oriole!' echoed Fulvia, and
this time the calm coolness of her voice
and expression changed.   'He lives with
you ?   How and why is that ?'

'Mia cara, after you were married—
the day you were married—he left Casa
Dietrich, never to return.   He was very
unhappy—so unhappy that it makes me
so only to think of it.   He quite disappeared for a time.   Even I lost him ;
and we are great friends, as you know.
Then almost by accident I found him
again, in a sad condition mentally and
morally, though he had become a little
better off as this world's things go.
Almost by force I brought him to
England with me.   I was leaving Rome

when I found him. He was to pay
me a long visit—that was all we said.
But my home has been his ever since
that day. He has never quite recovered
from that grief—your marriage, I mean ;
but I think, except for that, he is almost
contented. I think he is happier than
he would be anywhere else.'

' It was very kind of you,' said Fulvia,
in an abrupt, cool tone. She began to
beat with her parasol on the skirt of
her dress—the only sign she had given
of nervous discomposure. ' Is he very
sad ? Do you know, I think it will be
better to drop talking of all that time.
It is quite over and done with. I am glad
he is not in poverty. It would be very
delightful to be near you, and yet——'

' Don't decide upon anything. Think
about it.'

' I cannot say that I will not, though
I don't know whether I am wise to

consider it.   My   husband   always   had
a   sort   of   vexed   admiration   for   you,
because   you   had   an   assured   position
and were hardly civil to him.   He might
like   to   go   somewhere   where   we   knew
someone   who   was   " in   society " '   (with
another   little   cool   laugh).   ' But,   listen !
You   will   come   and   see   me,   won't   you ?
I am busy to-day—I have a lot of things
to   do ;   but   to-morrow   come   and   have
lunch   with   me   if   you   can.   After   lunch
I   will   take   you   to   see   my   husband.   If
I should find an opportunity between now
and then,   I   will tell him   I   have seen you,
and what you say about this place.   What
is it called ?   But you can tell him all that
yourself.   It   will   be   something   to   talk
about—the   greatest   boon   in   the   world
to me.'

' I   will   come.   You   must   give   me   your
address,'   said   Minna.   She   hated   the
idea of seeing Marchmont, but she could

not refuse Fulvia's request, and she felt
a kind of delighted joy in the fact that·
Fulvia wished to see her again—turned
to her with confidence, as an old friend
in whose goodwill she trusted.

'Yes. And now, I am sorry to say,
I shall have to go. I suppose the carriage will be waiting. Can I take you
anywhere? What are you doing?'

'Loafing about,' said Minna, laughing;
'and to some purpose, since I have met
you. No, thank you; go your own way.
I must join my friends at lunch.'

They rose and moved slowly away.

'Stop!' exclaimed Minna suddenly.
'Did Hans bring you here to see that
thing of mine?'

'Exactly.'

'And did he not mention his own
picture, hanging here in the corner?'

'No!' said Fulvia quickly, turning back
again. 'Where is it—and which?'

Minna pointed it out to her. Fulvia looked at it for some little time in silence. She did not smile, she did not frown, but turned at last to Minna, saying simply, though very gravely :

' It is very pretty—and very sentimental. He ought to do better than that, and he intends to.'

' Does he ?' They were now really walking away. ' To tell you the truth, I was almost more surprised to see him than you. I thought he was in the Tyrol, or Italy, somewhere, for the whole summer.'

' He was at Como when we were there a month or two ago. He was even then on his way home from Southern Italy and Sicily. He came to England about a fortnight after we did, and of course we have seen a good deal of him since. He knows everything, you see,' she added, in the same grave, matter-of-fact tone. 'We have some few acquaintances in London, and houses where we visited; but my husband is morbidly anxious that they should not know about our being here now. And yet he gets so nervous and fidgety if he has not some outsider to talk to. So Mr. Riemann's society has been a real godsend.'

'Yes, of course,' said Minna vaguely.

At the door of the gallery, Fulvia gave Minna her card and address, and held out her hand. She did not avoid her friend's eyes. She smiled most frankly and most sweetly upon her as she shook hands. It was Fulvia's old smile—outwardly. Holding her hand for a moment, Minna said:

'I shall be writing to Signor Oriole. I shall tell him I have met you. It would be absurd not to do so. Will you not give me some message for him?'

Fulvia's lips tightened for a moment. Then she said quietly:

'Please give him my love, and say that perhaps we may meet during the summer, if—supposing we should by any chance think of this place you have told me of.'

'Very well,' said Minna, and Fulvia added cheerfully :

'I am so glad he is independent now. It must make everything so much easier for him.'

With another pressure of the hand they parted. Fulvia got into her carriage, and was driven away. Minna, torn by all kinds of different emotions, kept thinking, 'How glad I am to have found her ! How I wish she would not keep saying she is glad he is independent, as if that compensated for everything else ! I shall see her again to-morrow. What is she in reality ? What has he become ? She is a riddle to me yet.'

Vaguely she went out into the street, looking about her with the equally vague

intention of getting into an omnibus to go
part of the way home, and finally, with an
impatient 'pshaw!' beckoned to the driver
of a hansom, got into it, and was like-
wise borne into the working-day world
again.

CHAPTER XVI.

AT a few minutes after half-past one on the following day, Minna rang the bell of the large, demure-looking door of a large, well-kept, and equally demure-looking house in a good street off one of the most fashionable squares. ' Lodgings,' perhaps, but evidently first-rate ones, both as to accommodation and, probably, price.

A man-servant opened the door. Mrs. Marchmont was at home. He led Minna upstairs to the drawing-room, announced her, and departed. It was a large, handsome, tastefully furnished London drawing-room, having very little about it of the usual serpent's trail. Fulvia rose from a low chair which stood beside a small table covered with newspapers and periodicals.

' It is very good of you to come. Put off your mantle—so. When I have a friend with me, I hate to see her looking as if next moment she would be going away. And your hat—so. You are not changed one bit, cara signora,' she added, with more warmth and approachableness of manner than she had yet displayed. Minna said little. Her heart was very full.

Fulvia led her to a sofa near the window, placed her there, and sat down beside her. She was exquisitely dressed in a sort of morning gown of muslin, lace and ribbons. One portion of her bargain at any rate had been kept, the side of luxury, of which Fulvia had spoken with assumed enthusiasm to Minna, when she had first made her her confidant on the subject of her engagement. There was a

sumptuousness in the young woman's entire
appearance which was carried out to the
minutest details of her attire and its ap-
pointments. Minna looked at her, and
her artist's eye, as well as that of human
affection, took it all in, and contrasted it
with the little blue woollen frock of former
days.

'We will have lunch first, and then go
to see my husband,' said Fulvia, and to
Minna, in whom the recollection of the
past was so vivid, it was a mystery how
she could utter those two words, 'my
husband,' and wear that slight, cool smile,
look at her interlocutor with those clear,
limpid eyes, and carry herself with such
unembarrassed ease.

Lunch was announced, and they went
downstairs. They were alone, and they
talked about a great many things. Fulvia
appeared to be very candid, very cheerful,
and very indifferent. She told Minna of

many things that 'they' had done at different times since her marriage. The only peculiarity which Minna noticed about her conversation was that it never referred to anything earlier than two or three years back. As to the first year or two of her marriage, or what she had done or seen then, or where she had been, she was absolutely silent, except that once she casually mentioned having been in Australia ; and when Minna incautiously asked when, she said, with a sudden freezing coolness of tone, ' Oh, it was about four years ago.'

They seemed to have passed a good deal of time at Vienna, perhaps the most absolutely frivolous capital in Europe, as Minna recollected. There, from Fulvia's account, they had met personages a good deal connected with politics and diplomacy, and she, at least, had made a success in rather exclusive circles. She spoke with

regret of not having been able to devote
herself to this life.

' I should like a political life,' she said ;
' I should like a political salon very much.
You see, anyone like me, young and
strong, and with an active, inquiring
mind '—she laughed a little—' with a great
deal of money and no children, is really in
need of something to do with her time.
There are several occupations and pas-
times which such a woman may take to. I
have thought of them all. She may go in
for society and utter frivolity, or for being
a *femme incomprise*, or for literature, or
art, or mysterious fascination, which means
lovers, or for politics. I have come to the
conclusion that politics are the least risky,
the most satisfying, and at the same time
the most exciting of these pursuits. And
I had just brought my husband round to
my way of thinking. He had decided to
settle in England, and look out for a con-

stituency. Of course he would have had to buy it, but those things can generally be managed ; we should have lived chiefly here, in London, and then—we should have seen. Just when it was decided, he was overtaken by this illness, and there is an end of it all.'

' Temporarily ?' hazarded Minna.

' Altogether. We shall have to live in the country, and I dread it, I must say. I have got so accustomed to excitement, of one kind or another, that I shall be very badly off without it. I do not deceive myself as to our position—not in the least. In London, people like us may conquer and hold fast a certain kind of standing—if we do not mind how much money we spend. In the country—in the county, which, of course, is the only part of the country worth considering—it is quite different. More difficult, slower, more subject to mortifying ups and downs than in town. No, I dread the country. It will be a *vera seccatura* to have to live there.'

Minna did not like the tone of all this.

But she had nothing to say to it. It all looked as if her little Fulvia had been hardened into a woman of the world; and if so, what wonder? Perhaps it had not been in her nature to be elevated by such an experience. Perhaps it was better that she should have developed into this, than sunk into a lifeless, spiritless thing, without nerve to meet her life.

Lunch over, Fulvia rose.

' I shall have to drag you upstairs,' she said. ' The whole of the second-floor is given up to him, and I have my bedroom higher still. This way !'

Silently Minna followed her, and they mounted the stairs to the second-floor. Fulvia tapped at the door of a front-room. It was opened at once by a man-servant.

'Is Mr. Marchmont ready to see us?' asked Fulvia. 'I sent him word I was bringing a friend.'

'Quite ready, madam. He has been expecting you,' said the man, throwing open the door and announcing her.

'Come, will you?' said Fulvia, looking back for a second towards Minna, whose heart beat uncomfortably fast as the recollection came rushing over her of the agony, the fainting, the despair she had witnessed five years ago ; of the exceeding bitter cry which had gone forth from the girl Fulvia Dietrich, before she had, all shivering with terror, but strung up to the last pitch of self-abnegation, left her mother's room to become Fulvia Marchmont. The scene would not go out of Minna's mind, in spite of the woman she now saw before her—well, strong, and full of life, and

most certainly not crushed, visibly at any
rate.

She followed, as she had been bidden to
do. Fulvia walked straight up to where,
with its head towards a large, pleasantly-
shaded window, stood a luxurious invalid's
couch. It was broad and soft, padded,
with the most cunning contrivances for
giving ease to limbs tired or diseased.
Over it was spread a quilted silken coverlet of some gorgeous Eastern pattern.
Under this coverlet was, presumably, a
human figure, because at the head of the
couch there was a snowy white pillow,
adorned with lace frills and ruchings ; and
on the pillow reclined a head. The head
must, in the nature of things, be connected
with limbs, but so small and shrivelled and
shrunken were those limbs that no outline
of them was to be seen under the billowy-
looking cover.

The face, which was turned in their

direction as they came in, was such a
strange, distorted, withered-looking little
countenance as Minna did not remember
ever to have seen before. The mouth was
drawn down at one side in a ridiculously
grotesque way. One eyelid had drooped,
and would not be raised. The eye that
still possessed its power looked eagerly
and suspiciously at them, with the glance
which Minna remembered so well—sharp,
mistrustful and restless. The rest of the
face she would hardly have recognised.
It was that of a premature septuagenarian
—of a septuagenarian who suffered, and
whose sufferings had wrought no good,
or nobility, or sweetness in his nature,
which, in fact, had been ruined and rotten,
and hopelessly warped, or ever the sufferings had begun.

'Good - morning!' said Fulvia, in a
clear, cool voice as she walked towards
him.

'Good-morning, my dear, good-morning. I thought you were never coming.'

He feebly stretched out his skinny little left hand, and held it towards her without paying any attention to her visitor. She just touched the hand with the tips of her fingers, and then, turning, said :

'Here is Mrs. Hastings. You remember her at Rome. She was very kind to me, and she did a bust of me—do you remember ? She has been having lunch with me.'

The grotesque head made a grotesque kind of inclination on hearing these words. Minna was forced herself to come forward and say :

' I am sorry you are so much out of health.'

'Oh, a mere temporary thing—a kind of sunstroke, or something of that sort,' said the voice she remembered so well. That was hardly altered at all. ' Where did you meet Mrs. Marchmont? Was it an accident, or did you know we were here?' he continued impatiently.

Minna was glad of the torrent of questions, which she proceeded to answer categorically.

He did not pay much attention to what she said to him, but continued to follow with his eyes every movement of his wife, as she moved hither and thither about the room. Minna began to realize something of the facts of the case. The man into whose power Fulvia had been sold while still a child was now a miserable, hopeless invalid, as helplessly in her power as she had been in his. She was strong. She had force of character and stamina of constitution. She had inherited her mother's strong will and her father's mental ability. She had got over the horrors and miseries of the first stage— slavery. The reins had now fallen into her hands, and she had grasped them firmly. She had not the least intention of letting them go. That she felt the faintest spark of affection for this wretched little mummy on the couch, even in this helpless invalid condition, Minna could not for an instant believe. Everything about her, in her attitude, her look, her manner, in the tone of her voice, in the deliberate calm glance she cast upon the face that so eagerly followed her every movement, spoke of the complete mastery she enjoyed, of the unlimited power she exercised. She had evidently conquered in the fight—there must have been a fight with herself as well as with him— conquered fully and without reserve. No victory is bloodless, either materially or metaphorically ; no possession is gained without a price having to be paid for it, sooner or later. At what price had Fulvia gained her victory ? Minna wondered.

What had she given up in return for the power she had acquired?

Such questions rushed vaguely and hastily through her mind, as she tried to reply to Marchmont's questions, seeing plainly that he was not listening, and that he thought her presence a frightful bore. Fulvia presently seated herself near to them, and observed coolly :

'I told you what Mrs. Hastings had said about there being a place near to her which was to let. I told you last night. Did you think about it at all?'

'A place to let—oh yes! Yes, I thought about it. It's such a confoundedly long way from London to where you live, Mrs. Hastings,' he said restlessly.

'No place in England is far from London now,' replied Minna. 'It only takes six hours—not quite as much by a flying express.'

'No—no; that's true. Fulvia seems to have quite set her mind on going to see this place. She says she's going with you when you leave London. When do you leave London?'

'In less than a week now.'

'Ah, well! if she says she will go, she will go,' said Marchmont; 'and, as she says, the more perfect quiet I have, the sooner I am likely to get well. It is very provoking to be laid up in this way.'

Evidently his thoughts were entirely centred on himself and his sensations. Fulvia, not he, would decide upon where they were to go in order that he might have the 'perfect quiet' he spoke of. They sat with him for half an hour, and then Minna thought she must go. Fulvia said she would go downstairs with her, but promised Marchmont to return and read the newspapers to him. Minna unwillingly exerted herself to shake hands

with him. He wished her good-bye with
a restless, wandering glance which settled
nowhere except on his wife.

The two women parted. Fulvia came
all the way downstairs with her guest,
a proceeding which, Minna instinctively
felt, was very unusual on her part. She
supposed she might take it as a compli-
ment, or even as a mark of affection. A
meeting was arranged for a few days
hence at the house of Minna's friends, and
Fulvia added :

' He was quite right in saying that I
said I should go with you to look at this
house. Would you take me ?'

' Wouldn't I, my dear! I wish you
would go there.'

Fulvia smiled.

' I really am thinking about it. Though
I haven't seen it, it is the first thing I have
heard of which has in the least attracted
me. By the time I see you again I shall

have made up my mind, and will let you know.'

' I think she will have made up her mind to come,' said Minna to herself, as she went away.

CHAPTER XVII.

MINNA had given Hans her address, and he one day called to see her. It was getting near the end of her stay in London.

Her first reflection as he came into the room was perhaps slightly irrelevant.

'How old is Hans now? Let me see: he must be twenty-eight at least. He might be anything, as far as looks go.'

He certainly might have been anything from twenty-eight to thirty-eight, because he was dark and grave, with a certain picturesqueness of figure and richness of colouring which made him look older than

he really was. There was nothing left in
him of that ingenuousness which she had
known in him when he had been a youth.
His movements had a certain slowness and
deliberation which was neither languor nor
effeminacy. His smile, very infrequent,
was delightful when it came, and it came
now as he drew near to his cousin Minna,
took her hand, and bent his fine dark eyes
upon her.

'I have been remiss, Minna. I wanted
to come before ; but when one has been
two whole years outside one's own country,
and returned to London, one is apt to find
a good deal to do—to put it mildly.'

'I can well believe it, and feel the
privilege of receiving any visit from
you. To tell the truth, I thought you
were booked to be abroad a good deal
longer.'

'I had vaguely thought about staying
longer. But I'm a vagrant—I got tired

of cloudless blue skies and endless un-
abashed sunshine, and all at once began
to long for some English damp and
greenness.'

' In London ?'

' I see you have not lost your old
trick of taking a fellow up pretty sharply.
No, not in London—at least, only at first.
I'm hoping soon to be in the country.
I shall spend the whole summer, at
least, in England, and I hope you will
let me come and see you before it is
over.'

' Surely.   I should think it very strange
if you went away without coming to see
me.   You don't know our part of the
country, either.   Yes, you must come.
Come when you like.   You must take us
as you find us—Signor Oriole and Rhoda
and me.'

' He is still with you, then ?'

' Yes.'

' Is it true that Mrs. Marchmont has an idea of going with you to look at this place near yours ?'

' Yes. We go together the day after to-morrow. She says it is to be only for one night.'

' H'm. She knows Oriole is with you ?'

' Of course she knows. Hans, I must congratulate you on your picture. It is odd that you and I should be hand-in-hand here, after Rome, isn't it ? Those old days, I see, remained in your heart as well as in mine. I felt quite a thrill when I saw it. I pointed it out to Mrs. Marchmont.'

' Did you ? What did she say ?'

' You are so popular now that I can afford to tell you exactly what she said. '' Very pretty, and very sentimental,'' were her words. '' He can do better than that, and intends to,'' '

Hans smiled slightly with eyes a little downcast, and pulled out the fingers of the glove which he had removed from his right hand.

'She has not grown sentimental, at any rate,' he said, with the faintest possible shrug of the shoulders.

'No,' said Minna slowly. 'You go there often, I suppose?' she added, almost abruptly.

'Oh no!' replied Hans, lifting his eye at once, and looking straight at her. 'Very little. She is frightfully particular. Of course there can be no sympathy between him and me, fiend that he is ; and she simply doesn't encourage men about the place. Of course I call now and then, so do a few others ; but none of us go as often as we should like to.'

He spoke with a grave simplicity which had something almost boyish in it, and which stirred Minna's heart to a warm feeling for him. Her expression at once became more cordial.

'You see,' he went on, 'there's no chaperon, no lady-companion, no nothing. She's all alone ; Marchmont said he would have no one of the sort about the house, so——' He shrugged his shoulders again.

Minna thought to herself : ' That is, she does not choose to have a chaperon. Of course she could have one if she liked. But she has no need of any such appendage. She is strong.' All she said was :

' Well, I dare say she is quite right. Then, Hans, you will let me know when you want to come and stay with me. It is a simple place, you know. Don't expect the luxuries of your father's palace down at Brighton.'

' Don't twit me with that,' said Hans vexedly. ' How I detest that place, Minna ! The horrible vulgarity of it, the smell of money, for it is nothing else. The girls—have you seen any of the girls lately?'

'Not very lately. Once or twice one of them has condescended to penetrate to our Northern wilds, and astonish the natives with her costumes, and her general tone of fashion and—what must one call it?—*disinvoltura.* But you know they are not bad girls. Their bark is far worse than their bite. It is their education.'

'I don't get on with them,' said Hans candidly. 'And they think me a mooning, sentimental idiot. So there is a great sympathy between us. The whole aspect of that place—the newness, the bareness, the glass-houses, and the gravel drive; the organ, and the picture-gallery, and—*tutti quanti!* No, I will promise you not to pine after it when I am with you.'

'Don't despise it, my good sir. It means ease and freedom from care for you in days to come. You are an artist now; you may be a Mæcenas some time.'

'I don't want to be either,' he said, drawing his brows together.

'Not wish to be an artist! Hans!'

'Well, not that exactly. We always want what we haven't got. My wishes I tell to no one.'

He rose to take leave. She did not detain him. He repeated his promise of writing to her, and departed. After he had gone she stood for a few minutes, thoughtfully looking down, her hand resting on the mantelpiece.

'I wonder if his wishes have any connection whatsoever with his picture,' she thought to herself, and shook her head. 'I hope not.'

＊   ＊   ＊   ＊   ＊

Fulvia kept her word, and met Minna at the railway-station on the appointed

day. She dismissed her servant, when he
had attended to her, saying :

'You can go, Parkinson. Be sure you
see Mr. Marchmont, and tell him it was
all right at the station, and that I will
send a telegram to-morrow to say at what
time you are to meet me. It may be
night.'

The man went away. Very soon the
two women were alone together in the
carriage, and the train speeding swiftly
Northwards.

They were not very talkative, but at
last Fulvia said :

'What did people think and say when
Signor Oriole became part of your house-
hold ?'

Minna shrugged her shoulders.

'My dear, what could they do or say ?
My well-known eccentricity was considered to account for everything. One or
two of them said it was very funny, but

I really did not care much what they said. Besides, I had my brother to support me in all that I did. He quite approved.'

' Your brother ?'

' Yes. I have one brother, and scarcely another relation in the world. His daughter, my niece Rhoda, almost lives with me. My brother is a man whom no one can despise or pooh-pooh. He is a very lucky man. He holds extreme opinions (so called) on many questions, social and religious and others, and yet he is accepted and respected as if he were the most orthodox of the orthodox. 'You know, I am a much more commonplace, conservative person than he is in reality, and yet I have the credit of being reckless, impulsive and defiant of all the conventionalities, while Mr. Hamilton, who despises conventionalities in a practical way which I dare not attempt, is a tame cat in the most rigorously respectable houses. Thus it is sometimes.'

'Yes, I know. What did he do, then— Mr. Hamilton—to make things straight?'

'My dear Fulvia, I cannot admit that they needed making straight. But if they did, this is how it was managed. Very soon after my return home with Signor Oriole, Richard came to stay with me, bringing Rhoda with him. He paid me a long visit. He was seen everywhere with Signor Oriole. They got on splendidly. We were all together constantly. My niece and your—and Signor Oriole are devoted to each other. His ways with children and young people are fascinating —there are no fathers so charming to their children as the Italian fathers. You have only to see them together to know that at once. Then we all went away together, and stayed a good while at my brother's place—in fact, we live alternately at each other's houses. I returned, with Rhoda and Signor Oriole. He has taught her Latin and Italian. There was really nothing to be said. I do not know a single friend of mine who really knows him and dislikes him.'

'No,' said Fulvia, in a low voice and with downcast eyes. 'To know him is to love him. If Beppo had had the destiny suited to him he would have been the adored father of the happiest family of children the world ever knew. I know it.'

She said no more about it, but something in her face told Minna that she felt all this more deeply than, perhaps, she would have admitted.

Minna was thinking of the coming meeting all the time that she was driving Fulvia in her pony-carriage from the station to her house, a distance of some six miles. They drove through the lanes, whose hedges were fresh with the brilliant green of early June, not yet white with hawthorn—that is a bloom which rarely shows itself early in Durham— clear-looking fields and pastures, great trees with polished leaves shining as they rustled in the wind ; along the highroads they drove, elevated and giving great sweeps of landscape, chiefly huge swells of moorland, purple under the changing sky, and in the far distance a silver shimmer which was the sea. The air was fresh and cool, the sun was bright, the pony was happy and willing. The six miles were quickly covered, and then they stopped in front of a small plain wicket from which a short footpath led to the deep porch of a long-fronted two-storied house without any claims to architecture. Windows had here and there been thrown out, to afford more room and more light, quite regardless of neatness or any effort at appearance. Different

kinds of roses clambered over the porch
and up to the windows, and a thick mass
of ivy covered all one side of the house.
At the sound of their wheels a gardener's
boy had come from some hidden region,
grinning from ear to ear, to hold the pony.
A waiting maid in a lilac print gown and
a white apron came flying forth from the
kitchen side of the house, smiling a
welcome.

' Take the things, Mary. Put that bag
in the blue room for Mrs. Marchmont.
Is Signor Oriole in ?'

' Yes, ma'am. At least, he was writing
in his study half an hour ago.'

' Come, Fulvia,' said Minna, gently
taking her hand, and leading her into
the house. The front door stood wide
open, showing a broad tiled passage,
square, like a hall full of shade, but with
rays of sunshine pouring down also from
a landing window at the head of a short

flight of shallow stairs. Minna paused a moment, and then said :

'You will come and speak to him at once, won't you ?'

'Oh yes, please,' replied Fulvia, almost nervously. 'At once. Then it will be done with.'

'This way, then. Shall I go away, and leave you with him ?'

'No, oh no, my dear Mrs. Hastings!' she exclaimed almost imploringly. 'Come with me, and stay all the time; I am strong, but I am not made of iron.'

'I will stay,' was all that Minna said, leading her along a passage, and through a sort of little anteroom to a door at which she knocked. A voice from within cried, 'Avanti.' Fulvia was pale as death, still and rigid. Without pausing, Minna opened the door and went in, drawing her companion with her by the hand.

Facing them, and just rising from his

place before a table covered with writing
materials, papers, and books, was Signor
Oriole, a white-headed, white-bearded man
with a pale face, but with thick eyebrows,
scarcely touched with the frost of years,
and flashing dark eyes, clear and brilliant
as ever, belying his look of age. Minna
felt Fulvia's hand spring aside within
hers. She divined the shiver of emotion
which must be shaking her soul ; she
quietly released the hand, and, blotting
out her presence as much as possible, said
simply :

'Here is Fulvia, signore.'

Fulvia stood, looking pale and rigid
still. Mechanically she allowed him to
take her hand ; they were both very
grave as they looked one another in the
eyes. Their last interview had been that
in which Oriole had offered to take Fulvia
away with him and hide them both from
her mother's iron resolution—that in which

his whole heart had gone to her, and in which she, white, trembling, agonized, but resolute, had strung herself up to refuse the offer—to stay, and take what should come. At parting she had flung herself into his arms with a wail of despair, and he had strained her to his heart and kissed her without a word. It had been the moment in which they had come nearest to flinging aside all concealment, but they had parted even then without the final word.

It could not be that moments such as that were not distinctly present in the consciousness of both. But now, after a few seconds of what seemed paralyzed silence, Fulvia's figure lost its rigid look. She smiled, just the same sweet, cool smile that Minna knew so well, and said :

' After so long we meet. It is only a week since I knew you lived here with Mrs. Hastings. Let me tell you, caro

signore, I find you look much better here
than you used to do in Rome.'

'Good heavens! Is that all she has to
say?' muttered Minna beneath her breath.

'And you, Fulvia, are indeed changed,'
was his reply, as he bent his eyes upon her
piercingly, but apparently without much
emotion. 'It is true, you have grown five
years older since I saw you—a long time
in a young woman's life.'

He lifted her hand to his lips and bowed
over it with courtly, old-fashioned grace.
They spoke quietly and steadily, but
Minna noticed that they both spoke
Italian, and addressed each other in
Roman fashion with *voi* instead of *lei*,*
and she drew her own conclusions from
these facts.

* *Voi*, you; *lei*, thee. The latter is the usual mode
of address when any politeness or formality is exacted.
The former betokens some familiarity, but is much
more used, even by acquaintances, in Southern than
in Northern Italy.

It did not last much longer. Minna made a move to leave the room, saying she would show Fulvia her bedroom, and send her a cup of tea there. They all moved away. The meeting was over. The emotions, whatever they might have been, had been well choked down, resolutely repressed from motives of common-sense and decent self-control.

Thus, under this foreign but friendly Northern roof, did the father and daughter meet—children of the South and of its hot impulses, eager quickness, passionate loves and hates—both beaten by circumstances into a demeanour and a conduct utterly different from that which would have been natural to them ; both, in spite of all the past, in spite of all that had been lived out and battled through by them, in spite of every attracting link of sorrow and suffering, ' strangers yet.'

CHAPTER XVIII.

THE visit was only as long as Fulvia had said it would be. Nothing that Minna could say prevailed upon her to stay two nights instead of only one. She passed the evening with her friend, and partly with Signor Oriole—that is, he dined with them, and joined them afterwards in the drawing-room for a short time, but afterwards went, as usual, to his study, to Minna's great disappointment. She had indulged in vague, dim ideas and hopes on the subject of this meeting, desiring that it should, somehow or other, bring Fulvia and her father together. It had apparently done nothing of the kind. They were civil to one another, amiable, pleasant, and nothing more. Neither seemed oppressed by the other's company, but, on the other hand, neither seemed anxious to be left alone with the other, or to be much together. It was perhaps quite natural, Minna owned with a sigh, as she saw Signor Giuseppe withdraw, leaving her and Fulvia together.

'I think you will be awfully tired, Fulvia, if you return to-morrow afternoon.'

Fulvia laughed.

'Tired. I am never tired. I am very strong,' she said, raising her head and throwing her shoulders back. 'To make fatigue an excuse for staying would be ridiculous indeed.'

On the following morning she went with Minna and her niece Rhoda, a rather awkward, 'leggy'-looking girl, with a promise of future good looks, on an expedition to the Hall, to look at it and judge of its suitability for their purpose. She said little, but that little was favourable. Coming back to lunch, she expressed herself satisfied with all she saw of it and its appurtenances. The solicitor of the family who wished to let it was in London, and from him she could obtain all necessary particulars.

'I shall give my husband a good account of it,' she said. 'I shall try to persuade him to come. And if we come, we shall come soon.'

When lunch was over, at which Signor Giuseppe was again present, the two women went together to Minna's drawing-room, where they were alone. Rhoda and Signor Giuseppe, who were the firmest of friends, went away, first to do a Latin lesson, and then to take a long country walk. Fulvia looked thoughtful as she seated herself, and said :

'Though he is so changed, he is just

the same as ever. He makes all the young people happy who come near him. I see it is the same with that niece of yours. I could find it in my heart to envy her.'

'He is assuredly very good to Rhoda. She is having a most unconventional bringing - up. Latin and Italian with Signor Oriole, some everyday grammar and geography and arithmetic with Mr. Howard, our old curate here. She gets some music lessons now and then. It is not her strong point. My brother teaches her something—a kind of social science, I think—and I——'

'And you?' asked Fulvia, with a smile.

Minna laughed.

'My department may perhaps be that which in the well-known dame's school was called, "Manners, twopence extra."'

'Rather more than manners, I think,' said Fulvia, 'if it is anything like what you did for me in Rome, so long ago.'

'Don't say I did it. I did what I could to comfort you, that was all. The root of the matter was in yourself, for it was only a short time that we were together. One could not tell then whether you were weak or strong. It seems strong.'

'Oh, I don't know,' said Fulvia carelessly. 'A great deal, I suppose, depends on one's circumstances. Perhaps if I had been exposed to poverty and struggle, and disappointments of that kind, I might not have been so 'strong' as you call it. Some natures are strong in one way, some in another. The fact is,' she went on, looking at Minna with the same open, candid smile, 'I was not born for poverty, Mrs. Hastings, nor for obscurity. I don't say it boastfully, but because I know it to be absolutely true. My mother knew my nature better than I did myself when she arranged my marriage.'

'Fulvia!'

'Well?' said Fulvia, looking calmly at her. 'You look appalled, amazed. What I say is perfectly true. I found it out— well, very soon after I was married; at the same time, in the same moment, I may say, as that in which I began to value my diamonds.'

'No,' said Minna in a tone of pain, 'you do not think so. You are saying it just for—for——' She stopped abruptly.

'Ebbene! For what?' asked Fulvia tranquilly. 'Do you not like me to say it?'

'I hate you to say it.'

'What would you prefer me to say? That I have been and am a miserable woman? That I was crushed by my lot? That I had not the power to meet my circumstances, and with a strong hand to control them, instead of letting them con- trol me? That is the only other thing that I could say. And yet you have just

been praising me for being strong, a kind
of praise which, I flatter myself, I deserve
to a certain extent.'

Again Minna was silent. Had she
spoken the truth, given utterance to the
feeling that was in her heart, deep down,
she would have said : 'Yes, I had rather
in truth have heard that your bravery and
strength were employed to conceal the
saddest of hearts, than that you had no
sadness to conceal. I would rather you
had been sad to the last day of your life
than that your conquering strength had
crushed, not only your adverse circum-
stance, but your highest and best self, your
soul, your heart. For that is what it
comes to when you say you are satisfied.
I do not wish you to be satisfied with
this.'

'I don't mind telling you about it,'
Fulvia went on. 'You were so kind to
me when I was such a silly, miserable girl.

I don't forget old kindnesses, and I should like you to know me as I am—no better and no worse. I was miserable for ever so long—worse than miserable, dark, wretched, despairing. Oh, it was awful, that hard, dry wretchedness that eats into your soul like some hideous corroding disease! I made up my mind at once to cut myself adrift from my old life, absolutely and entirely. I did not even write to Beppo, as you know. I had been made to do what I didn't want to do. We all hate that—naturally. I was vexed, cross, and even furiously angry. But I got over it. I found it was worth while to get over it, and that, on the other hand, to sulk and pout, and cry till my eyes were scarlet all round, and my nose like a beetroot, was not worth while. Do you know when I first felt that—that it was worth while to get over it ?'

'How can I know ?'

' It was at a great ball in London, at
a very grand house to which we had been
invited through an Australian Minister
then staying in London, who could not
afford to risk my husband's displeasure.
There was money in the question, of
course ; there always is,' said Fulvia,
smiling again. ' We went to this ball.
I was in a very bad humour. I had all
sorts of silly, sentimental scruples about
putting on my white satin and diamonds
and pearls—a lamb dressed out for the
sacrifice, a kind of Iphigenia, you know,
and all the rest of it. Dio mio! what
nonsense ! What a self-important, self-
conscious *bambina* I was! I had to go,
whether I liked it or not. I had been
crying in the morning, and my husband
was very angry with me. He had
threatened me with all sorts of vague
but terrible punishments if I did not,
as he called it, rise to the occasion and

pull myself together a bit. And I will tell you something else—a most ridiculous thing. I had just passed my seventeenth birthday ; the fearful and wonderful hours at which the entertainments began, to which we went, were a physical trial to me. Things are late in Rome too, of course, but, then, I hadn't been to any things, except occasionally. I was a mere child. I craved my sleep, my beautiful long, unbroken sleep that I had always enjoyed till then. Sometimes I used to fall asleep while my maid was dressing me for one of those functions, and had hard work not to do so when I got to them—not to yawn in the face of my partner at dinner or in a dance. This time, however, I was excited even before we arrived at —— House. It was all very new to me. I had never been at anything like that before. I was at first so shy and sad that I kept very

quiet, and was thus saved from committing some solecism or making a fool
of myself somehow. As the evening
went on, I found that people were looking
at me. I found that men were asking
to be introduced to me. They were such
wonderful men, it then seemed to me—
so utterly different from any men I had
ever seen before. I saw in their eyes
that they found me beautiful. They
talked to me, and when they found that
I had to keep eking out my still scanty
English with Italian, they were more
than ever delighted with me. Some few
of them spoke my native language more
or less badly—generally more so, I must
say. In short, I was a great success.
I was introduced to a Royal Personage,
who said some excessively commonplace
things to me, and was himself excessively
amused at my initiating several remarks ;
but he said he liked it, so my reputation

for charming originality grew apace. I felt that I was a person of distinction. My husband came up to me once during the evening, and whispered into my ear, "You will do. Keep it up like this, and I'll give you whatever present you like to ask for." I could not quite tell what it all meant, but it made my head feel gay and excited. It took me away from my miseries. It was pleasanter to think of than——' She shrugged her shoulders. ' Our home life was not altogether enchanting. During the evening I was dancing in a quadrille with a very handsome young Englishman, and just opposite to us was a countrywoman of his. She also was very handsome. I saw that she looked at me a great deal, but of course did not speak to me. I never made her acquaintance, though I often saw her afterwards. I don't know how one gets to know these things, but one always does.

I discovered that the season before she
had been one of the greatest beauties of
the` year. She had had a good many
offers, and amongst them one from my
husband, whom she had refused very unceremoniously. Now she was hearing,
or rather guessing, that on all sides people
were saying that Marchmont had married
someone more beautiful than she was.
And though she did not in the least regret,
I am sure, having refused him, yet she did
not like to hear—and to see—that his wife
did really surpass her in beauty. Yes,'
pursued Fulvia, ' it was that evening, in
the light of the hundreds of wax candles,
and amidst all the beautiful flowers, beautiful women, and fashionable or distin-
guished men at —— House, that I first
realized it was worth while to wake up,
to be strong, to preserve my beauty and
make the most of myself. I understood
it. It came to me like a revelation. That

was the life I was born for, and I was soon at home in it. It suits me, and I do not wish to exchange it for any other.'

'You have never had any children?' asked Minna quietly.

Fulvia started, surprised for a moment from her self-possession, and exclaimed, hastily and fervently :

'No—no! Thank God, I never had a child. And now—I never shall.'

'If the life suits you so admirably, it almost seems——'

'Che! I am woman of fashion. What do women of fashion want with children? Lovers, on the other hand——'

'Lovers! I hope you'll never condescend to that.'

'Oh, bah!' said Fulvia, with superb amusement. 'You don't suppose I mean love in a serious sense? That is ridiculous. I suppose it exists—but not for

people like me, not for people of my world.
It would only hamper us——'

At this moment the door opened, and
Signor Giuseppe walked into the room.

'May I join you, as Fulvia is so soon
leaving?' he asked.

'Oh, surely. Come in.'

He seated himself. 'Do not let me
interrupt you,' he said to Fulvia. 'I
heard your voice as I was coming in. Go
on.'

Fulvia hesitated a moment, looking almost embarrassed. Then, glancing down
a little, she went on :

'I was talking to Mrs. Hastings about
my life and my occupations. As I was
saying'—she looked again at Minna—
'falling in love would only be a great
hindrance to us in our career. You see,
everything is changed so—the relations of
men to each other, of class to class, of
order to order, and, above all, the relations

of man and woman to each other. And the relations of women towards society and towards the world are changing wonderfully. It is recognised everywhere now—at least, by all who have their eyes open—that women are henceforward to play a different part in the world's story. There is a class of woman now existing who will never marry, are never asked to marry, and are not a bit less happy on that account. And why? Because, though they will never marry, they have their clearly defined place in the world. There is a place for them now, though formerly there was none. They form one section, and a new one, of womankind—a sort of connecting link between men and women. I call them the third sex,' pursued Fulvia to her silenced but not delighted hearers. 'Then, again, there are the women who marry for love, for the purpose of living with their husbands in homes of their own, and having children, and perpetuating the practice and tradition of the great domestic virtues which are supposed to be so very firmly developed in this particular country.' She smiled a little, not very genially. ' They are valuable, too ; in fact, we couldn't very well do without them. But there are yet others who marry, sometimes consciously for position and influence and estate ; sometimes unconsciously— sometimes they have it thrust upon them.' She did not smile at all, and Minna felt that there was deadly earnest behind her calm manner. ' At any rate, they enter upon that condition, and then they find that there is a world for them, too—a place for them, too, in public affairs, in the social parliament, in giving its tone to modern life in general. Such women necessarily have numbers of—well, whatever you like to call them : admirers, hangers-on, lovers —it's an old-fashioned word. They know

exactly what use to make of such a state of
affairs ; they know that feelings, and love,
and all that kind of thing, are not for them.
They have quite a distinct sphere—an influence and a world apart from all senti-
ment—except what happens to be fashionable at the time ; and love no more enters
into their calculations than it does into those
of the women I first spoke of.   They wield
another kind of power.   It is better suited
to them, and better worth having—for
them.   In a vague, formless way every-
body knows this.   Some day it will be
formulated and written about, and reduced
to a system ; and by that time fresh de-
velopments will be in the air.   But sometimes one even of that order of women
forgets herself, and somebody teaches her
that she has a heart, and it runs away
with her, and then——'

'And then, there is the devil to pay,'
observed Signor Giuseppe, who had not

lived for five years in England without picking up some terse native expressions, which he used often with singular point and correctness.

'Exactly,' replied Fulvia with a light, hard laugh, as she shrugged her shoulders. 'It is because she is weak, then. She does not by nature belong to that order. The sooner that fact is proved, and she is relegated from it to another for which she is more suited, the better for her and everyone else.'

'I think your doctrine a hard one, and a heartless one,' said Minna, ever more and more constrainedly.

'But—exactly!' exclaimed Fulvia almost impatiently. 'Have I not just been saying that heart is for one set of people only? There are others who are happier and better off without taking it into account. Surely it is better that they should know this, and should get the best out of their lives that is to be extracted from them, rather than spend their time in struggling after some impossible ideal, and dying discontented and misunderstood ?'

Minna shook her head as she rang the bell for tea to be brought in. There was something wrong, fallacious and unreal about it, though it tripped glibly from Fulvia's clever tongue. The most painful thing about it, to her, was that she could not make out whether Fulvia spoke in jest or earnest, for effect, or from a fully convinced heart.

'Does your husband take any interest in all this ?' she asked suddenly.

'Oh, my husband's sole concern now is his ruined health, and his futile hopes of some time being well again. And in any case it does not much matter what he thinks about it. You know he was *roturier* to the backbone. He was nowhere in society. With all his money, he had no graces of his own with which to conquer a footing in it. It was I who did that for him,' she said, raising her head a little, and both, as they looked at her wonderful beauty, pure in its outline, girlish still in its freshness, refined and proud, felt that what she said must certainly be true. 'I won his place for him. It was for my sake that he was tolerated—yes, tolerated,' she repeated, coolly meeting Minna's eyes with unmoved calmness. 'He knows it. Ill though he is, he does not wish to sink out of that world which it cost him so much money to enter. He does not quite like never to be able even to seem to hold the reins, but he would dislike it still more if I were to drop them, and put on a cap and apron, and settle down to nurse him, and never leave his bedside.'

Everything that she said, with such tranquil, quiet assurance, bore upon it the

outward impress of truth. As Minna very
well knew, such lives, such circumstances,
did sometimes so adjust themselves, especially if the woman who was thrust into such
a position proved herself strong and self-possessed. A weakling, in the circumstances,
with this young woman's beauty, tempta-
tions and absence of safeguards, would
either have made some disastrous mess of
her life, or would have sickened and pined
away in sorrow. Fulvia Marchmont had
done neither the one nor the other. She
had strength of will and weight of brain,
which had been ripened and developed
with hothouse rapidity, very painfully and
very early. Was that all? was the
question which tormented Minna. Had
the gentleness of her girl's nature been
quite killed? Was there no weak or
vulnerable point, no bit of heart left un-
protected by the steel mail of worldliness
in which she had encased it? Was she

happy, having really found what suited
her nature and tastes and capacities? Or
was the extreme contentment, amounting
to complacency, at least half put on to
conceal a void 'behind the veil'? That
was what Minna could not decide to
her own satisfaction. The things which,
in the whole conversation, had most per-
plexed and disheartened her had been
Fulvia's quiet statement that her mother
had known best and decided wisely, her
utter, cheerful calm in meeting Signor
Giuseppe, and the bright, clear, dry glance
with which she looked into his face, with
its profound sadness—for profoundly sad
it was, despite the softening influences of
the last few years.

'I shall try one more test,' Minna
decided within herself, and after a little
while she said :

'You must not go away without coming
to see my particular den, Fulvia. Come

with me now. It is where I oftenest spend my time, so you will know where to think of me. Come with us, won't you?' she added, taking Signor Oriole's hand, and drawing him along with her. They went through the hall to the other side of the house, where were two or three moderately sized rooms opening one out of the other.

' Here is my sanctum,' said Minna. ' I don't do any more sculpture now—nothing to speak of. That is the almost last real piece of work that I finished — really finished, you know. Do you remember it ?'

She pointed with her finger to the bust of Fulvia the girl, and led Fulvia the woman up to it, and made her stand in front of it.

For a moment her lips twitched, her eyebrows contracted. She did not speak for some time, but stood quite steadily and

motionless before the bust, her hands
lightly folded one over the other. At last
she said :

' I am sure it was an excellent likeness.
I can see my present features exactly.'
She smiled, and drew her forefinger down
the line of her nose. 'And the eyes and
the forehead, and the way the hair grows
—it is myself exactly, even now. But the
expression ! Did I really look such a woebegone, sentimental, lackadaisical creature
as that ?'

She laughed, and turned inquiringly to
Minna, who replied in a slow, sad voice :

' Yes, you looked even so sad as that ;
and you felt even so sad as that.'

Again a little impatient shrug of the
shoulders, and a smiling ' Dio mio ! I must
have been a very depressing companion.'

She turned to find Signor Giuseppe
standing just behind her, gazing with intense, wistful earnestness through his

spectacles, alternately at her and at the likeness. His face was full of some kind of emotion. She resolutely declined to notice it, but said to Minna :

' I think it is an awful pity that you do not work any more at such things as this. If you had been a poor woman you would have had to do it, and you would have earned name and fame.'

' Possibly,' replied Minna dryly, as they went out of the room.

Fulvia would not sit down again. She said it was high time to get ready for her drive to the station, as she would not miss the train on any account.

*　　*　　*　　*　　*

She had gone, almost promising to return and bring her husband to Yewridge Hall. Minna, back again in her own house, went straight to her den, threw aside her hat and gloves, sat down in a chair directly in front of the bust—the

work of her own hands—and looked in-
tently at it, interrogating it, entreating it.
So sad—so unspeakably sad and grieved—
that girl's face! So firm, so bright, so
apparently untouched by grief or care, un-
troubled by any wish save for power, and
conscious pleasure in possessing a great
deal of it, that of the woman! Yet the
cold marble, with the look of one who was
sad unto death, was not really as lifeless as
the living woman, who smiled and talked
and spoke brightly and took a superficial
interest in all that was going on.

Minna started, and her eyes dilated.
Had she at last got the clue to the trans-
formation? What were the words that
tried to take shape in her mind as she
looked at the immovable marble, and
thought of the marble endowed with life
now on her way to London? The name
of an old play, the words of some old
proverb—' Killing no Murder.'

' That is it !' she exclaimed aloud, and then, looking again and again at the sweet sad lips which she herself had carved, she said in a whisper to herself :

' No, it is worse than that ; it is murder no killing ! That is the answer to the enigma ; I know it is. It was her own mother who did it. Oh, horrible, horrible ! She murdered, without killing her ! Her soul is dead—that's what it is—poor little Fulvia's beautiful soul and warm, beating heart—murdered ; while her body and her brain are left to live on alone. How I used to wonder, just after she was married, how it would end, what turn it would take with her—crush her, or harden her, or kill her ! It has been the moral death. She is murdered, and is yet living.'

There are moments in the lives of most of us in which some great truth comes home to us with overpowering force. It may be

uttered by other lips, and may from them
strike straight into our souls, as the
answer to some strange and puzzling
problem over which we have been brood-
ing. The sight of a picture ; the notes of
a song, or of some instrument of music ;
the prospect of clouds in the heaven, or
rain sweeping across the fields ; the wail
of the wind on a stormy day or night :
any or all of these may, with a lightning-
quick flash of intuition, crystallize the idea
which has been floating in a state of
solution in our minds. Such intuitions
have the value of spiritual revelations —
they are beyond proof; they may even be
disproved theoretically—they can never be
the less true and real to those who have
experienced them ; and although every
voice on earth should uplift itself and
pronounce them false, it were useless. He
or she who has been thus, as it were,
smitten in the face, in the heart, and in the

soul, by one of these flashes of spiritual insight, never more has the power to disbelieve it.

Such a revelation came at that moment into the heart of Minna Hastings, as she sat with her hands clasped round her knees, and looked up at her own handiwork, standing on its pedestal, and gazing forth with nameless sadness into life.

Minna had never had a child of her own; she had, however, above all things, a mother's heart, and craved with unspeakable craving for motherhood. All children and young things were dear to her : they all loved her and confided in her. She had known many girls since her own girlhood ; had heard from their own lips the histories of their griefs and joys, their hopes and fears ; had loved them, counselled them, admonished them, been patient and kind and helpful to them ; but she had never loved one of them with

such a love as that which she had borne to
Fulvia Dietrich.   Of all the girls she had
known, Fulvia was the one whom she would
most have desired to be her own child.   It
swept over her heart now, this deep love,
like a great wave, strong as ever, pitiful,
yearning as ever, and she knew how
Fulvia's lot had saddened her own bright
life.   She realized what that sudden meeting with her had meant.   As she looked
and looked, her sadness increased, till it
was almost more than she could bear.
Great tears gathered in her eyes, fell from
them, rolled down her cheeks and into her
hands, and before she knew what was happening she was shaking with sobs—the
sobs of an endless pity and compunction,
the sobs of one who would fain help to
overthrow some great wrong, heal some
immense grief and injustice, and who
cannot.

Without her being aware of it, the door

of the room had been opened by someone who had knocked twice and received no answer. It was Signor Giuseppe, who came in and first made her aware of his presence by laying his hand upon her shoulder.

'Why are you weeping?' he asked in a husky voice. 'I could not wait any longer. Why do you weep? Has she been complaining? Has she told you her griefs?'

'No,' said Minna sadly. 'I wish she had; it would have been better. I should have felt happier if she were crying all day, than that she should have become what she is. You will see; you must know what I mean.'

'I know what you think,' he said slowly.

'And don't you think the same?'

'I don't know. We shall see, as you say. She practically promised me to come here.'

' Promised you ?   When ?'

' I saw her alone for a few minutes,' he said with a smile.   ' It was before lunch —before she made that brilliant dissertation to you on the subject of women and their spheres.   I diritti della donna,' he added with a little laugh.   ' It sounded very well.   She is a brave girl, that Fulvia! She will come here and be near us.'

But Minna, looking at the marble like-ness of Fulvia Dietrich, shook her head, and her heart misgave her.

END OF VOL. II.

BILLING AND SONS, PRINTERS, GUILDFORD.